ROYAL AUDACITY

A Novel

MOGOR OBIORAH

ISBN: 9798844382871

Imprint: Independently published

To the memory of my sister

MRS. JOSEPHINE NKECHI MORAH

CHAPTER ONE

On the eleventh day, in the seventh month, after the demise of *Igwe* Okaaomee, members of the council of kingmakers of Ogiga kingdom gathered in the residence of the regent of the town, to deliberate on some pertinent issues affecting the development of their town. The Igbo people In West Africa call their kings, *Igwe.* The council of kingmakers was made up of all the members of the prestigious *ozo* society, and representatives of all the villages that made up Ogiga kingdom. Head of the *ozo* society was the regent of the town; and he was also the president of the council of kingmakers; while Isi-Ichie, who was the head of all the titled men in the kingdom, played fatherly role to them.

The indigenes of Ogiga Kingdom were accommodating and peace loving; their major occupations were farming and fishing. Beneath the ground in the town was large deposit of black gold, crude oil which was supposed to be a blessing to the people ... but the reverse was the case; because international oil companies that operated in the kingdom often embarked on oil drilling and extraction without regard to global best practice. Oil spillage that was a regular occurrence in the kingdom, threw many indigenes of the town out of job; because their farmlands were often submerged by oil and the rivers were polluted, and that made the fishes and other aquatic creatures to die.

Ogiga kingdom had a king that ruled them and served as interface between the community and the government etcetera; but the ultimate power resided with the people; and Isi-Ichie held this power in trust for the people. Selection of Isi-Ichie was divine, because before anyone was installed as Isi-Ichie, he must have to be the oldest man in the town.

Isi-Ichie was the highest authority in Ogiga kingdom. He had the responsibility of crowning and suspending the king; whenever the need arose. He maintained balance between the king and President-General of Ogiga development union; and no one could transact any business with the name of the town or on behalf of Ogiga people without his knowledge and consent.

Ogiga kingdom practised gerontocracy up until the coming of the colonial masters. It was in a bid to please and relate properly with the colonial masters that the people of Ogiga kingdom created the office of a king. *Igwe* Okaaomee was the twenty-fifth king of the kingdom; and he ruled his people with the fear of God for a period not less than forty years before joining his ancestors at the ripe age of eighty. Customarily, no new king should mount the throne of their ancestors until a year after the town must have organised the last ofala festival for the dead king. Ofala festival was an annual royal ritual in their own geographical location and last Ofala festival was often organised for a dead king; though the nomenclature was different in some towns.

Selection of a new king in Ogiga kingdom was always combustive and volcanic, because external forces always tried to influence the outcome of the process. The state government often wanted a king that would be amenable and loyal to it; while the international oil companies often sponsored any candidate that would turn the other way while they plundered the land and destroyed the environment. Build up to the final selection process was always characterized by intrigues, mayhem, arson, murder and kidnapping.

While the council of kingmakers meeting was going on in the regent's residence, Okoro stood up and took a swipe on the kingmakers for neglecting what seemed like the most important responsibility of the council of kingmakers. All the members of the council of kingmakers were present at the meeting except Isi-Ichie.

Okoro chided his colleagues for not putting in motion a process for the selection of *a* new king for their people despite the fact that date for their late king's last *ofala* festival was fast approaching. He equally informed them that their people would be expecting them to present to them the potential King during the last *ofala*. Moreso, he told them that tongues had started wagging; and that people had started doubting their competence. "I want to suggest that we start searching for who would be our next *Igwe* now! Before it is too late," he concluded and sat back on his chair. Among the Igbo people of West Africa, a king is called *Igwe*.

Uka stood up immediately ... observed all the necessary protocols; and then went ahead to state that they had a system that made it easier for them to select and present a new *Igwe* to the people at the appropriate time. "From the way Chief Okoro sounded, I believe he has someone in mind. Fellow kingmakers, I solicit we ask Chief Okoro to tell us that person he feels is fit to be our next *Igwe.*"

Uka's assertion pleased the other members of the council of kingmakers; and they concurred.

"That's all I have to say," Uka said and sat down.

Okoro took the floor again and informed the gathering that he knew quite well the tradition of their town and the procedure for selecting a new *Igwe.* He equally opined that his mind was agitated by the pace at which everything in the world moved at supersonic speed. He went further to say: "I think it is high time we joined the bandwagon; and move along with other towns ... by selecting and installing as *Igwe,* someone that is dynamic, robust, rugged, influential, wealthy, educated and widely travelled. If I am allowed to recommend ... I have someone in mind."

"You're free to recommend," said Iloka.

"Empty your mind before us Chief Okoro," Afoka added.

"Since you have the interest of the town at heart, go ahead and tell us whom you want us to choose as *Igwe,*" said Oji.

Oji's contribution gladdened the hearts of some of the chiefs; and they nodded in agreement.

"If I still reason aright," Okoro stated, "I think Obi, the son of Nwako is fit to be our *Igwe.* His achievements in life and the numerous philanthropic projects he has done in this town makes him the most suitable person for the job," he concluded.

"You're absolutely right Chief Okoro!" Okeke shouted, from his seat.

"That is all I can say at the moment," Okoro said and lowered his buttocks on his seat.

Ndu was the regent of the town ... he rose from his seat and shouted greetings to the kingmakers in the traditional Igbo way. The kingmakers equally responded in the traditional Igbo way.

"*Ibe anyi kwe nu!*" Ndu shouted with agility.

"*Yaa!*" others chorused.

"*Ka chaa nu!*" Ndu shouted again.

"*Yaa!*" others chorused again.

"*Biri nu!*"

"*Yaa!*"

Like Okoro, Ndu said glowing things about Obi Nwako; and added that Obi Nwako was more than qualified to be the king of Ogiga kingdom. He further said that anyone with contrary view needed to see a psychiatrist. "But we should not be in a haste in deciding who should be our next *Igwe* [king]; and neither should we allow compassion and sentiment to blur our sense of judgment."

Some of the chiefs muttered something while others nodded to show support to Ndu's assertion. Ndu was not done; he took the attention of his colleagues to the constitution of their town. "The constitution of our town states that *Igwe* is the custodian of our culture." He equally said: "And for anyone to qualify to stand for selection as our *Igwe,* such person must be a member of *ozo society,*" Ndu added. "I don't know if Obi Nwako is yet an *ozo* title holder," he concluded.

"Obi Nwako is not yet an *ozo* title holder," said Okoro.

"I rest my case," Ndu said and took his seat.

"If being a member of the *ozo* society is the only hurdle Obi Nwako needs to cross, ... he is rich, he will get himself initiated into the *ozo* society soonest," said Okoro.

"Until he becomes an *ozo* title holder, he's not fit to be considered for the throne of this kingdom," Ndu retorted.

All the other members of the kingmakers looked at each other and shrugged.

A convoy made up of a Rolls Royce and a jeep came into Okoro's compound and parked. The compound was lonely; the only sound heard in it at that moment was the noise being made by birds that chirped on trees that dotted the compound and the neighbouring compounds. Two armed policemen came down from the jeep with the driver whose name was Amadi; together they hastened to the Rolls Royce. John, who was the driver of the Rolls Royce came down and opened the door to the owner's side. Obi Nwako came down from the Rolls Royce ... and moved toward the main entrance to Okoro's house with his drivers and the two policemen that came with him. The worried and ruffled looking Obi Nwako tapped and opened the door to Okoro's house; he went into the house while the others waited outside. The two policemen sat by the entrance door the moment Obi Nwako shut the door, while the two drivers went and dusted their vehicles windscreens.

Okoro welcomed Obi Nwako to his house and offered him seat in his sitting room. Obi Nwako thanked his host before taking the weight off his feet. Okoro sat down too and expressed delight in having the privilege to host Obi Nwako. "Excuse me," he said; ... he stood up and was rushing to get kolanut for his visitor.

"Forget about kolanut, Chief Okoro."

Okoro halted and looked at his guest with a face laden with surprise. "Why?" he asked.

"I'm not in the mood."

Okoro went and sat back in his seat; after staring at Obi Nwako for some time, he comported himself and asked: "I hope all is well?"

"Chief ... there is fire on the mountain," was Obi Nwako's response.

Okoro sensed that there was problem; he adjusted his sitting position and requested that his visitor told him what was bothering him.

Obi Nwako stared into space for a while and heaved a sigh. "Chief."

"Yes," answered Okoro.

"You informed me that the council of kingmakers resolved to crown me as the next *Igwe,* if I'm initiated into the *ozo* society."

"Yes, I can remember telling you that," Okoro said, while nodding.

"I have started the process."

"That's good to hear."

"But ... a mountain has refused to get off my way; despite pleas from myself and others."

"And what could that mountain be?"

"My kinsmen refused to consent to my request for initiation into the *ozo* society."

Okoro looked at Obi Nwako from head to toe, laughed wryly and asked: "Is that why you're upset?"

"Yes," replied Obi Nwako, "I can now see the Promised Land, but the red sea has consistently and adamantly refused to part for me to step across."

Okoro chuckled and asked Obi Nwako not to entertain any fear. He went further to assure him that the red sea must part for him to step across to the Promised Land. "Every Pharaoh, every Egyptian, every Herod and Goliath that conspired and vowed never to allow you have a fulfilled destiny must bow, because a superior power is coming to crush them."

An elated Obi Nwako shook his head and shouted an ecstatic, "Amen!"

Okoro was not done yet, after praying for his friend, he went on to give him an unparalleled hope. "The regent and all the members of the council of kingmakers have resolved that you will be our next *Igwe.* I'll tell them the problem you're having with your kinsmen and at the same time ask them to impress our decision on your kinsmen; so that they will consent to your desire to become a member of the prestigious *ozo* society."

Obi Nwako looked up, heaved a sigh; and while beaming, he said: "I will be happy if that works out."

"Just count on me, and sleep well whenever you have to."

"I knew that with you on my side, I can attain to any height in this town."

"Exactly," said Okoro.

Before Obi Nwako left Okoro's house that day, he gave huge sum of money to the latter; and promised to give him more financial reward, if he convinced and get the members of the council of kingmakers to make things easier for him, or bend the rules for him if need be. Okoro asked him to count on him; he went on to promise that he would never rest until his guest was crowned king of Ogiga kingdom.

A week after Obi Nwako's visit to Okoro's house, Ndu sat in the garden that was in his compound reading newspaper and licking oranges. After sometime, his gate opened; he looked toward the gate and saw Okoro coming into his compound. Okoro was delighted when he saw Ndu seated in his garden; beaming with delight, he walked toward the latter. Ndu stared as his guest approached the garden. They shook hands and exchanged pleasantries when Okoro got closer. Thereafter, the host offered seat to his guest before sending for a bottle of wine and two wine glasses. While they were waiting for the wine and wine glasses, Ndu asked after Okoro's wife and son.

"I thank God for his kindness toward us," was Okoro's response.

Okoro had visited Ndu some days earlier and intimated him of the problems Obi Nwako was having with his kinsmen; and pleaded with Ndu to intervene and pressurise Obi Nwako's kinsmen to consent to Obi Nwako's desire to be a member of the *ozo* society. Ndu agreed to step into the matter and promised Okoro that he would meet with the head of Obi Nwako's kindred to find out why they were averse to their son's progress. It was the outcome of Ndu's meeting with the head of Obi Nwako's *umunna* [kindred] that Okoro had gone to find out. Deep down in his heart, he felt that coming to ask Ndu how the meeting went was a mere formality, because he believed he knew what the outcome of the said meeting would be. He was of the view that Ndu's personality would intimidate Obi Nwako's people and force them to consent to Obi Nwako's desire.

A bottle of wine and two glasses were brought to the two men at the garden, as requested by Okoro's host. Ndu prayed over the wine before opening it. As they drank the wine, Okoro sought to know if Ndu was able to meet with the head of Obi Nwako's kindred. Ndu responded in the affirmative; but Okoro was shocked by the outcome of that meeting. Ndu told him that Obi Nwako's kinsmen still did not agree to give their consent to Obi Nwako's application for initiation into the prestigious *ozo* society.

"Did they bother to tell you their reasons for taking such nasty decision against their son?"

Ndu shook his head and told his guest that getting Obi Nwako to be the king of Ogiga kingdom was as difficult as getting a hen to pee.

"You seem to have lost me," said Okoro.

"First, they said he's ten years younger than the minimum age requirement for initiation into the *ozo* society."

Okoro got irritated and said: "That's nonsense! Are they his mother? ... How did his kinsmen know his real age?"

"Chief Okoro, the issue is much more than what you think it is."

"I don't understand."

"Again, they said they knew where Obi Nwako started and how he started; but they did not know how he got to where he is today."

"Meaning?"

"They suspect that he made his money through dubious means."

"My regent, in my own view ... since all the members of the council of kingmakers and the majority of our people want Obi Nwako to be our king, I want to suggest that we over rule his kinsmen or bend the rules and crown him; in consonance with the wishes and aspirations of our people and thereby enthrone everlasting peace in the land."

The regent laughed wryly and opined: "For as long as I, Chief Ndu remain the regent of this kingdom, the rules cannot be bent to favour anybody. I'm not prepared to die before my time."

"It has not gotten to that," said Okoro.

"Going contrary to the tradition of this kingdom is suicidal. Our custom demands that before one is initiated into the *ozo* society, such a person must have attained a certain age, and he must be of proven integrity; and these must be attested to by the applicant's kinsmen."

"I know all that," said Okoro.

"Can I ask you a question, Chief Okoro?"

"Go ahead and do that," Okoro said.

"Do you think you love Obi Nwako more than his kinsmen ... that you feel they are being unjust to him?"

Okoro told Ndu that under normal circumstances, he was not supposed to love Obi Nwako more than his kinsmen would love him. He went further to tell Ndu that they must not dither in acknowledging that some people are wickedly jealous of other people's success.

"Obi Nwako is most qualified to be our king. Let's amend our Kingship constitution and recommend Obi Nwako for coronation."

Ndu made it emphatically clear to Okoro that their tradition required that it was persons of impeccable character that would ascend to the throne of Ogiga kingdom. As a way of buttressing the point he made earlier, he went further to let his guest know that that was why their ancestors stated in a rule, "that before anyone should dream of becoming the king of Ogiga kingdom, such person must first of all be a member of the prestigious *ozo* society."   Okoro was disappointed by what was coming out from the regent's mouth. What he was hearing were different from what he had expected to hear. Ndu noticed his mood, but that did not deter him from telling him the truth. "As regards the amendment of the Kingship constitution," said Ndu, "I'll advise you to table it in the next meeting of the council of kingmakers."

"I'll gladly do that if you'll oblige me," said Okoro.

"Why not?" asked Ndu. "I will oblige you," he assured his guest.

"I will be grateful if you would allow me to move for the amendment of the Kingship constitution," Okoro stated in a tone that suggested that he was skeptical of Ndu's earlier promise.

Okoro's host tried very hard to allay his fears. He reminded Okoro that every member of the council of kingmakers had the right to state his opinion or make suggestions during the council's meeting. Okoro appeared not too convinced, but he heaved a sigh when the regent emphatically assured him that no one would stop him from moving a motion for the amendment of the KIngship constitution of Ogiga kingdom.

Council of kingmakers meeting was convened in Ndu's residence few days after Okoro's last visit to the former. Attendance for the meeting was same with that of other meetings of council of kingmakers held in the same venue. During the meeting, Okoro stood up to address his colleagues. He indulged in circumlocution; and spent several minutes drifting from point to point; and from idea to idea without saying categorically what he wanted. His lack of direction and coherence made those listening to him worried and uncomfortable. "My fellow chiefs, as I have said many times before now … based on the exigencies of the time, and in order to avert this looming danger from befallen our kingdom, I plead that we join the bandwagon of progressive and development oriented societies."

"Okoro say what you want and sit down; so that we leave here in time," said Ndu.

Okoro apologised for wasting their time; lowering his head he said: "My regent, my fellow chiefs, I am sorry if I am taking much of your time. In our last gathering, in this same place, we all agreed that Obi Nwako is most qualified to be our next king."

The other chiefs nodded to show that they concurred with Okoro's claim. The chiefs' concurrence to his claim gladdened Okoro's heart and boosted his confidence. He went on and tried to woo them to his side with the hope that his colleagues could be easily swayed. Going forward, he informed them that provisions in the Kingship constitution placed insurmountable hurdles before Obi Nwako. Furthermore, he told them that there was need for them to align with the wishes and aspirations of majority of their people … that wanted Obi Nwako to be crowned as the king of Ogiga kingdom. "With regards to the foregoing, I move for the amendment of our

Kingship constitution, so as to make it possible for Obi Nwako to emerge as our next king."

From his seat, Agbakpo angrily shouted: "Sit down!" He stood up and shouted again, "Okoro sit down! if you don't have any reasonable thing to say."

Okoro was shocked and inert; he turned, looked Agbakpo in the face and asked: "Are you all right?"

"Okoro," Agbakpo called; touching his chest, he emphatically said: "I, Agbakpo *dike izu nke mbu n'*Ogiga kingdom has just asked you to sit down if you don't have something reasonable to say."

Agbakpo's command to Okoro was a catalyst for commotion in the meeting venue. Some of the chiefs stood up and supported Agbakpo, while others threw their weight behind Okoro.

"Silence! ... Silence!!" shouted Ndu with a voice laced with anger and disappointment. "Will you all shut up and behave yourselves. You're all chiefs for crying out loud."

As a mark of respect, all the chiefs complied with Ndu's directive by shutting their mouths and sitting down one after the other ... but Okoro and Agbakpo remained standing. They stared at each other panting and fuming.

"Chief Okoro."

"My regent," answered Okoro.

"Sit down there!"

Okoro looked at Ndu for a while before he disdainfully sat down.

"Better," said Agbakpo.

"And you too; Agbakpo *dike izu* ... Sit down there!"

Agbakpo sat down. Ndu continued, "I'm highly disappointed in all of you. Your behaviour in the past few minutes, smacks of irresponsibility. And I want to believe that such will not repeat itself again."

The chiefs apologised for their untoward behaviours. Ndu accepted their apologies and reminded them that their Kingship constitution stated that the regent should rule the kingdom for a period not less than a year... if the council of kingmakers failed to select a king for Ogiga kingdom before the last ofala festival of a dead king.

"As the sitting regent, I am not interested in ruling this kingdom. I want us to select a king and present same to our people as soon as possible. This council has rules, anyone that has something meaningful to say should quietly and gently stand up and make known to us whatever he feels is best for this kingdom."

Iloka took the floor and saluted the regent and his fellow chiefs with a bow. Thereafter, he made it clear to them that he would not be part of anything abominable. "Count me out of the sham called constitutional amendment. What did not happen in my father's time will not happen in my own time." He shook the dust off his feet and ... "I take my leave of you people."

Ndu closed his eyes and brooded for a while. By the time he opened his eyes again, Iloka had taken some steps toward the gate. "Chief Iloka!" he shouted, in a stern voice.

Iloka halted and turned.

"Come back here and sit down," ordered Ndu.

Iloka fumed and grudgingly went back to his seat.

Afoka stood up and saluted the regent and his fellow chiefs; he cleared his throat and looked round before making his own contribution. While making his contribution, he opined that change was the only thing that was constant in life; and that he could not oppose change, and neither would he be afraid of change. "But I, Chief Afoka will advise that we apply caution as we try to tinker with anything that might affect the future of our land. Let us be careful. Let us not allow sentiment to blur our sense of judgment," he concluded and sat down.

Uka rose and saluted his colleagues before making his views on the issue under consideration known. "I, Chief Uka ... I have nothing much to say; but I want us to ponder over this question: Why are we changing or amending our kingship constitution?"

All the chiefs were taken aback by Uka's question. As they looked at each other in amazement, Okoro looked toward Agbakpo; his eyes met that of Agbakpo. While the duo disdainfully stared at each other, Uka concluded thus: "That's all I have to say."

When it was Oji's turn to speak, he said: "I, Chief Oji ... I want to suggest that we tread carefully. Let us always remember that a wise man seeking to know the depth of a river does not put his two legs in the river at the same time."

Every member of the council of kingmakers that attended the meeting that day spoke either for or against the amendment of the Kingship constitution, except Okeke. All the other members looked expectantly at Okeke with the hope that he would voluntarily say something, but Okeke appeared unconcerned. The other chiefs looked at each other and murmured.

Ndu stared at Okeke and called ... "Chief Okeke."

"My regent," answered Okeke.

"You've not said anything," said Ndu. "What is your take on the subject under discussion?"

Okeke jumped up from his seat and cleared his throat, before telling his colleagues that they must not forget that they were members of the council of kingmakers because their people found them worthy, and strong enough to defend and protect the custom and tradition of Ogiga kingdom. He emphatically told them that there was need for them to be careful ... and apply wisdom before taking whatever stand that they might take. "Let us not do something that might set this kingdom aflame in the future. That is all I have to say."

While Okeke sat down, his colleagues looked at each other ... "Good talk," they murmured to one another. Pin drop silence enveloped the meeting venue while the kingmakers pondered on the point raised by Okeke.

When Ndu cleared his throat, all the kingmakers focused their gaze at his mouth expecting him to tell them why he wanted them to pay attention to him. He thanked all of them for their lofty contributions; and went further to ask if any of them had something more to say. He later adjourned the meeting when no other member indicated interest in making any further contribution. "Everyone should go back to the village he represents and consult widely and thoroughly on the issue at hand. We shall reconvene in a month's time to take decision on the matter. You may all rise."

The kingmakers rose from their seats ... as they bowed, they chorused: "The wish of the regent is our command."

They later brought the meeting to a close with a short prayer. Thereafter, they dispersed in small groups; chattering as they walked out of the compound ... to where some of them parked their cars at the front of Ndu's compound.

CHAPTER TWO

Okoro was whistling while he was happily driving home from the venue of the council of kingmakers meeting. Though the meeting did not endorse his prayers, he was happy that some of his fellow council members saw reasons with him; hence he believed that he only needed a little more effort to push his demands through. When he got to the gate to his village, he sighted Obi Nwako's convoy coming from the opposite direction. He smiled and flashed his car's head lamp before pulling up.

Obi Nwako's Rolls Royce and a jeep pulled up too. Beaming with smiles, Okoro came down from his car; and moved toward Obi Nwako's convoy. Two armed policemen came down from the jeep and moved closer to the Rolls Royce. Obi Nwako alighted from the Rolls Royce and exchanged pleasantries with Okoro. After the duo had finished greeting each other, Okoro told his friend that he was coming from the venue of the council of kingmakers meeting. Expectantly, Obi Nwako had interest in what Okoro said; he became apprehensive and sought to know what they agreed on at the meeting. Okoro smiled and confidently told him that he was already seeing a little light at the end of the tunnel. Okoro's claim and assertion could not satisfy Obi Nwako's curiousity; because of that, he besieged the former to tell him exactly all that transpired at the council of kingmakers meeting.

"I prayed them to amend the Kingship constitution so as to pave way for your emergence as our next king."

Okoro's claim whetted Obi Nwako's interest; and prompted him to demand that he be told more. Okoro pretended to be paying obeisance to him. Bowing down, he shouted: "*Igwe-e-ee!*" That is the way the Igbo people greet their kings.

"Chief, tell me, what did they say when you requested for the amendment of the Kingship constitution?"

"As expected, some voices dissented, while others supported the motion."

"And what happened next?"

"Well, the regent in his infinite wisdom asked us to go home and consult the people we represent in the council. We shall reconvene in a month's time to decide whether or not to amend the Kingship constitution."

"We're making progress then," said Obi Nwako.

"Trust me. We must triumph. I must get all the council members to support your aspiration."

"Chief, I have to allow you to go home and rest."

"That's very thoughtful of you."

"I shall see you later, so that we solidify our plans," said Obi Nwako.

"That's all right."

Okoro gave his friend a hug, turned and headed toward his car, while his friend entered his Rolls Royce and shut the door. The two policemen hastened to the jeep. Okoro zoomed off... and Obi Nwako's convoy followed suit, but that was after the two policemen had gone into the jeep.

Obi Nwako paid Okoro a visit about a month after they met on the road. It was eve of the scheduled meeting of the council of kingmakers. The duo had met a fortnight earlier. During their meeting two weeks prior, they fine-tuned the strategy they would use to get majority of the members of the council of kingmakers on their side. The prospective king was in Okoro's house to fulfil his own part of the bargain, as agreed upon by both of them in their last meeting. Okoro was happy that Obi Nwako did not forget that they agreed to meet on that day. After the kola nut ritual, they chatted for a while before Obi Nwako pulled closer a "Ghana must go bag" that was by his seat and told his host that they must not leave any stone unturned.

"We must be venomous in our strike," he said and pushed the bag toward Okoro. "Chief, our actions must be swift. In that bag is ten million naira. Use it to woo majority of the chiefs to our side."

Okoro, who was also the secretary of the council of kingmakers, smiled after he unzipped and inspected the content of the bag pushed to him by Obi Nwako. "You really know the language our people understand. With this money, the battle is as good as won."

 Obi Nwako was confident that the money would do the required magic; he equally told Okoro how much he believed and trusted in his skills and influence within the council of kingmakers. "Work with the money sir, and let's see how far we can go with it."

Okoro nodded; smiled and eulogized Obi Nwako for some time. Thereafter, he said: "You are the true son of your father."

They hit the back of their right palms together for three consecutive times before giving each other a robust handshake [because that's the way titled men of Igbo stock greet].

Okoro went to Obi Nwako's house to see him barely forty-eight hours after the former played host to the latter. The visitor looked gloomy and worried; he was with the same bag and the money brought to him by Obi Nwako during his last visit to his [Okoro's] house. His worry grew when he was told that Obi Nwako was busy. His friend's aide offered him seat in the sitting room, and he waited for a long time before Obi Nwako came downstairs to meet with him.

"My chief," said Obi Nwako.

Okoro turned and saw his host coming toward him.

"My distinguished chief," Obi Nwako said again.

Okoro rose from his seat and said: "*Igwe* [king] in the making. I remain loyal."

The duo greeted each other in a traditional way.

"You are welcome sir. Please sit down."

"Thank you," Okoro said and sat back in his seat.

"What do we offer you, sir?"

"I don't feel like taking anything?"

"Why? Is anything the matter?"

Okoro shook his head and hissed. *"Agwo no n'akirika,"* [There's problem] he responded.

"What is the problem this time around?" asked Obi Nwako. "Wasn't the money enough for the chiefs?"

"The money was rejected by all the chiefs."

Okoro's last statement surprised and got Obi Nwako agitated. "Why did they reject the money?" he asked. "If the ten million naira is too small for all of them, I can increase it to twenty million naira or even more than that."

"That's not the issue," said Okoro.

"Then, what is the issue?" asked Obi Nwako.

"They claim they occupy position of honour, hence they cannot sell their conscience for a mere plate of porridge."

"This is serious."

"It is more than serious," retorted Okoro. "I brought back the ten million naira."

Obi Nwako heaved a sigh and slid into deep thought. "Truly, there's problem," he said and shook his head. He held his cheeks with his hands and tapped his feet on the floor for some time before he emphatically asserted, "There must be a way out."

"I pray so," said Okoro who stood up almost immediately and begged to take his leave.

Okoro and Obi Nwako had never-say-die spirit. The duo never allowed the rejection of the bribe money by the kingmakers to deter them in their quest to get the kingmakers to support Obi Nwako's candidature for the throne of Ogiga kingdom. They had strategic sessions and brainstormed ... mapped out the possible and the easiest approach they would use to enlist the support of at least two-third of all the members of the council of kingmakers.

They later decided to go for the jugular.

The duo visited Ndu with the "Ghana must go bag" that contained the ten million naira that they had wanted to use in bribing the members of the council of kingmakers. Ndu welcomed them to his house. Thereafter, he presented kola nut and wine before them.

 "Doing justice to kola nut presented to visitors is the responsibility of the host," said Okoro.

The simple interpretation of Okoro's assertion is that their host should break the kola nut because it wasn't customary for a visitor to break kola nut presented to him by his host. Ndu picked the kola nut and offered a short prayer before breaking it. They began to do justice to the wine after chewing the kola nut. While they drank the wine, Okoro chose to break the silence. He told their host that they decided to pay him a visit because Obi Nwako deemed it necessary to pay him homage.

Obi Nwako told the regent that he had come to salute him for his wisdom and the excellent way he had been running the affairs of the council of kingmakers; and the entire kingdom since the demise of their king. Ndu told him that he felt flattered; he went on to add that he wouldn't have done all the good things people talked about without the grace of God.

At this juncture, Obi Nwako decided to tell him his main reason for coming to see him. "You may have heard ... but

I've come personally to intimate you of my desire to be the next king of our great kingdom. I am equally using this opportunity to seek your support."

Ndu chuckled and said: "You don't need to beg for my support. Every son of the soil will always have my support for every good thing they desire."

Okoro gave Obi Nwako a nudge; the latter stood up and pushed the "Ghana must go bag" toward their host. "My regent," said Obi Nwako, "in this bag is ten million naira. It is for your kola."

Ndu unzipped and inspected the content of the bag and smiled. Obi Nwako smiled back thinking that the smile he saw on the regent's face meant that the man had accepted the money; and he equally believed that the regent was comfortable with his desire to be next king of Ogiga kingdom.

"All these for me?" asked Ndu.

"You deserve it, my regent," responded Obi Nwako.

"That's very thoughtful of you. This shows you're wise and qualified to be the next *Igwe* [king] of this great town of ours.

The regent's assertion gladdened Okoro's heart; and he retorted: "There's no doubt in what you said, my regent."

"My regent, I want you to see this as a token," Obi Nwako said with pride. "Many more will come your way as soon as I'm crowned."

Ndu stood up and furiously berated his visitors for coming to bribe him. Okoro and Obi Nwako appeared shameful and disappointed in the regent. They shook their heads and became downcast. But their host was not done, he went on to tell them that coming to bribe him was an affront on him and the office he occupied. Furthermore, the regent asked Obi

Nwako how he would regard him and the kingmakers if he should accept his bribe and make him king. He equally sought to know if Obi Nwako would have any regard for the indigenes of their town if he should succeed in buying the crown.

"And you Chief Okoro, you are the secretary of the council of kingmakers; in my absence, you superintend over the council of kingmakers. You knew he was coming to bribe me; and you encouraged and even brought him to my house."

Okoro wanted to defend himself, but Ndu was not cut out for whatever defence he wanted to put up.

"Well, incase both of you do not know," said Ndu, "I am a man of proven integrity; a man of unquestionable means and a man of impeccable character. Now! ... Both of you should get up at this instance and get out of my house before I lose it."

"Hey my regent," said Obi Nwako, "it has not gotten to that. We mean no harm."

"I know you mean no harm; that's why I'm sending you out of my house in peace and not in pieces."

Okoro had his face buried in shame. He was deeply troubled because things turned out the way they never anticipated or imagined. Prior to their visit to Ndu's house, they were confident that they could easily buy the regent over, since he had said it severally that he was not interested in overseeing the affairs of their kingdom as acting king. Hence Okoro and his friend felt that the regent would be happy that someone like Obi Nwako had volunteered to wear the crown and save him the stress of sitting on the throne of his ancestors in an acting capacity for a period not less than a year.

The Kingship constitution of Ogiga kingdom stated that in a situation whereby the council of kingmakers failed to select a potential king prior to the last ofala of a dead *Igwe,* that the regent should hold firm to the reign of power for a period not less than one year; so as to allow the kingmakers ample time to choose and present a new king to the people. The constitution equally stated that in a situation whereby the kingmakers failed to select a king for the kingdom on the expiration of that initial one year, that the regent should continue to act as the king until a new king was crowned. But Ndu made it clear to members of the council of kingmakers that he was not interested in acting as their king. Hence, he wanted his colleagues to do everything humanly possible and select a potential king for the kingdom before the expiration of the time allowed for such.

Because Ndu did not want to be an acting king ... and because he wanted a potential king to emerge as quickly as possible, Okoro thought he would easily accept Obi Nwako and railroad his emergence as the potential king of Ogiga kingdom. While reacting to Ndu's expression of disappointment over the attempt to bribe him, Okoro said: "We came in peace my regent, don't be harsh on us."

"Chief Okoro, I know you came in peace; that's why I'm sending you away in peace. Or ... I'm I no longer your regent?"

"You're still my regent," said Okoro.

"Good, as your regent, I am commanding you to get out of my house; now!"

The visitors rose and were about leaving without the "Ghana must go" bag.

"Come back and carry this useless bag and money."

They turned and lifted the bag that contained the money they had come to bribe Ndu with; dragging the bag along, they headed for the door.

"I am made ... and I am comfortable and contented. I don't need your bribe money."

As Okoro and Obi Nwako exited his sitting room, he hissed ... "Nonsense," he muttered and sat on one of the seats that adorned his sitting room.

Visibly worried Okoro and Obi Nwako came out from Ndu's house, with the bag in which they stashed the money with which they had wanted to bribe the regent. They halted at the porch; dropped the bag on the floor and stared into space with uncountable hisses. After some time, Obi Nwako shook his head and broke the silence. "We're in a fix," he said.

"You're right. We're absolutely in deep shit," said Okoro.

"What do you suggest we do next?" asked Obi Nwako.

"I don't know. I am bereft of ideas at the moment," said Okoro. "But I think we need to think strategically and execute our plans tactfully."

"My hope is beginning to wane," said Obi Nwako.

"You'd better be hopeful for we must conquer."

Obi Nwako hissed. "Let's go," he said.

They lifted the bag and began to move to where Obi Nwako's convoy of two vehicles was parked in Ndu's compound.

John, the Rolls Royce driver and Amadi, the jeep driver were standing by the two vehicles chatting with the two armed policemen. John sighted Okoro and Obi Nwako struggling toward them with the bag. He abandoned those he was chatting with ... rushed and collected the bag that contained the ten million naira from the duo. The two friends felt relieved when the driver collected the bag from them and moved with ease with it. John flung the bag into the Rolls Royce; and after that, Obi Nwako and his friend entered the Rolls Royce and shut the doors through which they went into the car. Immediately John opened one of the front doors of the Rolls Royce; and sat on the driver's seat, Amadi and the two armed policemen entered the jeep ... and the convoy quietly left Ndu's property.

Ogiga council of kingmakers converged in Ndu's residence for mother of all meetings, two days after the regent disgraced the duo of Okoro and Obi Nwako out of his house. All the members of the council were present, and as usual, Okoro, who was their secretary, took minutes during proceedings. The meeting commenced with an opening prayer. After the opening prayer, the minute of their previous meeting was read and adopted. Ndu stood up afterwards and addressed the gathering.

He started by welcoming his colleagues to the meeting. Later on, he reminded them that in their last meeting, he charged them to go back to their respective villages and confer with the people they were representing; so that they could find out whether the people wanted the Ogiga Kingship constitution amended or not. His colleagues concurred; and he went on to express believe that they perfectly did what they agreed on. Again, the chiefs nodded; and hummed in the affirmative and began to chatter.

Ndu watched his colleagues for a while and cleared his throat. The chiefs muted their voices and paid attention to their leader.

"Without wasting much of our time, let's proceed with the voting," said Ndu.

The chiefs adjusted their sitting positions.

"Now, lend me your unreserved attention," said Ndu.

Pin drop silence enveloped the meeting venue immediately the regent requested for his colleagues attention.

"Those in support of the proposed amendment to our Kingship constitution should please indicate by raising up their hands," the regent requested.

Okoro raised up his hand instantly, but he shamefully brought it down when he noticed that his hand was the only one up. While Ndu meticulously observed his colleagues, the other chiefs mockingly urged Okoro to raise up his hand well and be counted. On the prompting of the other chiefs, Okoro reluctantly raised up his hand for the second time; but he shamefully brought it down again almost immediately.

"Based on the strength of my observation, I, Chief Ndu Onyechi, the regent of Ogiga kingdom, hereby turn down every request for the amendment of our Kingship constitution. Our constitution remains intact and operational. I have spoken."

All the chiefs rose ... Okoro thundered, albeit reluctantly, "The voice of the regent!"

The other chiefs chorused: "The voice of the people."

"You may all sit," said Ndu; and as all the chiefs sat down, he continued, "Based on the foregoing, I want all of you to go to your respective villages and get nominees for the position of *Igwe* [king]. We must receive their names on or before the day of our next meeting. All things being equal, we shall begin to screen them as soon as we receive their names."

All the chiefs, except Okoro were happy that at last the ceiling had been lifted for them to search for the person that would sit on the throne of their ancestors as successor to *Igwe* Okaaomee. Ndu's directive sounded like victory for justice in the estimation of the chiefs; hence, they shook hands and congratulated each other. Thereafter, motion was moved for the adjournment of the meeting. They later prayed and dispersed.

Okoro drove back to his house and parked in the car port. Looking devastated and disappointed, he walked to the balcony, fell to a seat and brooded for a while. After some time, he shook his head and hissed; before using his mobile phone to make call to Obi Nwako.

Obi Nwako was happy to receive the call; he requested from his friend, a detailed account of proceedings at the council of kingmakers meeting the moment he confirmed that his friend, Okoro was in the meeting.

"I was the only one that voted for the amendment of our kingship constitution," said Okoro.

"And what happened next?" asked Obi Nwako.

"The regent overruled the motion for the amendment of the constitution and implored us to go to our respective villages and get nominees for the position of *igwe* [king]. We shall start screening them in our next meeting."

"Impossible!" exclaimed Obi Nwako. "No one else can occupy that position except me."

"Have you any idea up your sleeve?" asked Okoro.

"Time will tell," was Obi Nwako's response.

Obi Nwako dropped his mobile phone as he panted and fumed. Okoro kept saying: "Hello," over the phone ... but he got no response from his friend. After some time, he began to hear Obi Nwako muttering, "Time will tell." Okoro kept shouting, "Hello," thinking that his friend, Obi Nwako would respond but that never happened. He heaved a sigh and ended the call.

Ndu, the regent of Ogiga kingdom was an honest man who wanted the best for his people. He was among the few people in Ogiga who believed that having a good name was better than wealth acquired through dubious means. He wanted posterity to remember him as a man that fought and preserved the custom of Ogiga kingdom. But little did he know that while he desired to move his town forward, some evil men were busy planning to disgrace him; twist his arm and even hijack the entire process from him.

Okoro and Obi Nwako were among those that vowed to sabotage any process that would lead to the selection of a new king for the people. Both men swore never to leave any stone unturned in their quest to have Obi Nwako crowned the king of Ogiga kingdom. Ndu underrated these men; he didn't take seriously all their antics until their scheduled meeting for the collection of names and screening of nominees and aspirants for the position of *igwe* [king] of Ogiga kingdom.

The meeting of the council of kingmakers commenced on a happy note with Okoro, the secretary of the council taking minutes of proceedings in the meeting. Ndu was happy because they were to kick start [in that meeting], a process that would throw up a new king for Ogiga kingdom. His joy was truncated when he requested the chiefs to turn in names of nominees and aspirants from their respective villages.

The chiefs wore sullen faces when they were asked to submit their respective lists of nominees and aspirants to their secretary. The regent was surprised, his eyes moved from one chief to another. The chiefs were uncomfortable, but Okoro was very happy. Ndu wondered if the chiefs did not do what he beseeched them to do. But, with the exception of Okoro, all the other chiefs claimed they did what they were asked to do. The regent heaved a sigh; and noticed that Iloka's hand was up. "Chief Iloka," he said, "you're raising up your hand ... let's hear what you have to say."

Iloka stood up and told them that two illustrious sons from his village declared interest in the race. "But they later changed their minds," he concluded.

"Why did they change their minds?" asked Ndu.

"They said there was serious threat to their lives."

"Who was threatening them?"

"That's what they didn't tell me, my regent."

"It's all right. You may sit down."

On the prompting of the regent, Okeke stood up immediately Iloka's bum touched his seat.

"My regent, my fellow chiefs, I salute you all," said Okeke. "I would have come with names of three nominees, if not that their families asked them to back down."

Ndu was bewildered by the reason Okeke gave as the cause of his inability to bring any name from his village. "Why would their families ask them to back down?" he asked.

They said some anonymous fellows promised to kill them or their loved ones if they remained in the race," said Okeke who sat back on his seat immediately.

"Hmm, terrible," said Ndu. "Yes, Chief Oji, let's hear from you."

Oji stood up and said: "One person from my village declared interest; but he chickened out after receiving threat calls from faceless individuals."

"Okay," said Ndu.

Oji bowed and sat down.

Ndu brooded for a while and then called on Agbakpo to give his own account. Agbakpo stood up and scratched his head for some time. "My regent," he said, "well to do men in my village declined interest. They cited fear of the unknown as their reason."

"That's all right," said Ndu. "Let's hear from you Chief Uka."

Agbakpo sat down on his seat while Uka stood up almost immediately.

"I salute you my regent," said Uka. "Everyone in my village is afraid. They said they don't want to die before their time."

"Lily-livered fellows," said Ndu. "I wonder whom they're afraid of."

"My regent, they're equally afraid of the assassins' bullets," responded Uka.

Ndu signaled Uka to sit down; the latter thanked him and complied. Ndu breathed out heavily and muttered: "God, what is our society turning to? ... Chief Okoro, you seem to have been indifferent and happy since this meeting commenced."

"I am not happy my regent," said Okoro. "You can see that I've been engrossed in my work as the secretary. I have been taking minutes since we started this meeting."

"Is there anyone from your village you would want us to make the *igwe* of Ogiga kingdom?"

Okoro stood up and answered thus: "All the people in my village are content with their present status. None of them wants to be the *igwe*."

"Sit down," said Ndu.

Without wasting time, Okoro acted as he was commanded by the regent.

Ndu tapped his foot on the ground and nodded like a lizard. He looked confused, worried and worn out. After he had slid into a deep thought, he coughed and told the members of the council of kingmakers that there was problem. That was not all, the regent went on to remind his colleagues that the last *ofala* festival of their late *igwe* was less than one month away. Going forward, he stated, "We must not forget that all eyes shall be on us on the day of the last *ofala* festival of *Igwe* Okaaomee who joined his ancestors some months back. Our people shall on that day expect us to show them the one that shall sit on the throne a year after the last *ofala* of our late *igwe* [king]. In whatever we do, let us be reminded that the next king of Ogiga kingdom is supposed to proceed on a year-long isolation, ritual and tutelage which shall commence twenty-four hours after the last *ofala*; and then end on the eve of his coronation as the *igwe* of Ogiga kingdom. And his coronation must take place a year after his predecessor's last *ofala* festival. If we fail to present the would be *igwe* to the people on the last *ofala* of *Igwe* Okaaome, I will be asked to sit on the throne in an acting capacity, a year after the last *ofala* of our deceased king. I don't want to act as *igwe*. I want us to do the right thing now."

Without wasting time, Uka put it to Ndu that the custom required the regent to ascend the throne and act as *igwe* for a period not less than a year if the kingmakers failed at anytime to select someone suitable to be the king of Ogiga kingdom.

"That has not changed," he concluded.

"Chief Uka, I have said it before, and I want to repeat it again … I don't want to be king or acting king."

"Why?" asked Uka.

"My family and my business still need hundred per cent attention," answered Ndu.

"Regent, you have no choice here," said Agbakpo. "The custom requires that you act as *igwe* for one year; and that is what you must do. Within that one year, we will be able to give our people a new *igwe* and choose his coronation date."

Agbakpo's assertion did not go down well with Okoro; but all the other chiefs were okay with that. Ndu took a deep breath and reflected on all that his colleagues had said; thereafter, he requested that motion for adjournment be moved. When motion for adjournment was moved and seconded … he declared the meeting closed, after the closing prayer was said by one of them.

Ndu could not sleep at night due to the kingmakers' inability to convince their people to declare interest in the throne of Ogiga kingdom. He was so worried to the point that his wife became disturbed; she stayed awake and worked very hard to talk her husband out of the worry and the hopelessness that had enveloped him. He was equally agitated because the Kingship constitution of their kingdom stated that he would be made the acting king of their kingdom if the kingmakers failed to present the potential *igwe* [king] to the people during their late *igwe's* last *ofala* festival. It sounded ridiculous to some people that he was rejecting something that many people were praying for. The likes of Obi Nwako was ready to do anything; even kill somebody in order to smoothly ascend the throne that Ndu was rejecting. His condition became a source of concern to his wife. She warned him against excessive thinking lest he contracted a sickness that he would not find palatable.

"In a worst case scenario," said Ndu's wife, "you ascend the throne, rule for one year and hand over to whoever the kingmakers will later choose."

"You don't get it dear," said Ndu.

"How do you mean? After all, the kingship constitution wants you to rule for just a year; if the kingmakers fail to choose a successor for late *Igwe* Okaaomee?"

"Dear," said Ndu, "in practice, that one year will definitely stretch to two or more years."

"How?" she asked.

"If the kingmakers fail to present the successor to *Igwe* Okaaomee to the people during the last *ofala*, they will make me the acting *igwe,* a year after the last *ofala* of late *Igwe* Okaaomee."

"And you will reign for just a year and hand over," said Ndu's wife.

"I hope you have not forgotten that whoever is chosen by the kingmakers will have to go into isolation for one year."

"I cannot forget that," was his wife's response.

"Within the one-year isolation period, he will have to undergo some tutelage, so that he will learn the things that will help him discharge creditably, his responsibilities as the king of Ogiga kingdom," said Ndu.

"I know," said his wife.

"Good. Let me now clear your doubt."

"I'm listening," she said.

"Well," he said, "my acting as the *igwe* for just a year is improbable. How long I will act as the king will depend on how soon the kingmakers will find *Igwe* Okaaomee's successor."

"Anyway," said his wife, "let's hope and pray that some persons will declare interest in the throne, before the last *ofala* of our late *igwe*."

"That has been my prayer," said Ndu.

"Can we go to bed now?" she asked.

"Sure," answered Ndu.

CHAPTER THREE

The sound of *Ufie* music rented the air; *ufie* music is synonymous with royalty and affluence. The royal arcade was filled with people. The crème de la crème of the society were there. Representatives of the state government and the international oil companies that operated in Ogiga were equally present at the arena. The commoners, women and children etcetera were there too. Ndi-Ichie were there with their wives; the wives of *ozo* title holders and that of the other members of the council of kingmakers were also represented at the event. And ... the event was the last *ofala* festival of the late *igwe* of Ogiga kingdom. People sat according to their status in the society and according to the group they belonged to. Those that did not belong to any group sat in unmarked part of the pavilion that was in the arcade and under some unmarked canopies; while some others that could not find seats stood beside and behind the canopies that dotted the arena.

The master of ceremony was dancing to the melodious *ufie* music while the journalists that attended the event were busy taking note of happenings in the arena. Also, videographers and photographers that came for the event were busy taking shots of all the actions taking place at the venue. The chief priest and his dwarf aide strolled into the arena barefooted; the master of ceremony punctuated his dancing escapade to announce the arrival of the man they called, "The mouthpiece of the gods." The chief priest nodded at the master of ceremony and went and sat on the seat reserved for him; while his dwarf aide stood behind him.

A convoy of eighteen vehicles came into the arena. The convoy was led by a sedan that had flasher on its roof; the vehicle that was at the rear of the convoy was a police van. The flasher on the sedan's roof was on and the sedan was being followed by a coaster bus that had a royal insignia on its body; the inscription, "ROYAL COUNCIL," was also boldly written on the body of the bus. Behind the bus were about fifteen vehicles that belonged to some members of the council of kingmakers. The fifteen vehicles were all chauffeur driven; and the members of the council of kingmakers in them wore white apparel, likewise those in the coaster bus.

"The royal council is here," said the master of ceremony.

The convoy came to a halt at the middle of the arena; four armed policemen jumped down from the police van and took positions at the four vertices of the arena. Also, two dwarfs came down from the sedan and moved round the arena with the intent of making sure that danger was not lurking around. Satisfied that the arena was free from negative spiritual forces, the two dwarfs went and stood by the door to the coaster.

All the members of the council of kingmakers that were in the fifteen vehicles that queued behind the bus began to come down one after another, while the two dwarfs remained standing by the door to the coaster. As the kingmakers moved closer to the bus, one of the dwarfs opened the door to the coaster. Regent and twelve other members of the council of kingmakers came down from the bus. The convoy left the centre of the arena ... all the members of the council of kingmakers moved toward the part where seats were reserved for them. *Igba-eze* troupe provided royal tune for them as they moved on.

"This is Chief Ndu Onyechi, the regent of Ogiga kingdom, flanked by members of the council of kingmakers," said the master of ceremony. "In case you do not know … the regent will act as our *igwe* for one year if the kingmakers fail to present an *igwe* designate to us today.

While the master of ceremony was still talking, the kingmakers' wives came out and welcomed their husbands; thereafter, they danced with the men to the pavilion and canopies were guest etcetera were seated. Everyone in the pavilion and canopies except Ndi-Ichie, stood up to show respect to them when they got closer. Ndi-Ichie was a group made up of old men that were eighty years and above. The position of Isi-ichie was the exclusive preserve of the oldest amongst the Ndi-Ichie.

Ndu shouted greetings to the people in the traditional Igbo way.

"Ndi be-anyi ka chaa nu!" shouted Ndu.

"*Iyaa-aa!*" shouted all the people.

"*Biri nu!*"

"*Iyaa-aa!*"

"*Umu unu zua unu.*"

"*Iyaa-aa!*"

The regent smiled confidently and said: "*Akanri* [right end]."

"*Anyi nwe* [belongs to us]," responded the people.

"*Aka-ekpe* [left end]."

"*Anyi nwe* [belongs to us]."

"*Ebe anyi si ka-odi* [whatever decision we take]," he said.

"*Ebe afu k'oga-adi* [shall remain as we have agreed]," responded the people.

"I thank you all," he said and moved to greet the chief priest and the important dignitaries that graced the occasion. As Ndu greeted and exchanged banters with the chief priest and some of the guests, most of those that were hitherto standing sat down while the kingmakers' wives went back to their seats. Members of the council of kingmakers sat down after exchanging pleasantries with many that came to witness the event.

Ufie music players began to give them tunes again; the master of ceremony shouted with joy and dashed to the middle of the arena and activated some funny dance steps with which he entertained the audience. The people clapped and cheered the master of ceremony for his mastery of the art of dance; but their enjoyment was cut short when Isi-Ichie was chauffeur driven into the arena. The master of ceremony signaled the *ufie* music players to stop producing tunes the moment Isi-Ichie's car crept into the arena. When *ufie* music stopped; the master of ceremony picked his microphone and announced the arrival of the Isi-Ichie. "Ladies and gentlemen," he said, "it is my honour to announce to you the arrival of the Isi-Ichie. May we all ri-se."

All the people in the arena stood up ... later on, Ndu, members of the council of kingmakers and Ndi-Ichie began to move toward the direction of Isi-Ichie's car. The master of ceremony raised his microphone and said: "The regent is leading the kingmakers and Ndi-Ichie to welcome the Isi-Ichie. You all know that in this kingdom, we operate a mixture of monarchy and gerontocracy."

Ndu opened the door to the seat on which the Isi-Ichie sat. Everyone in the arena including Ndu, Ndi-Ichie and members of the council of kingmakers bowed their heads the moment Isi-Ichie stepped out of the car. Standing by his car, the nonagenarian said a little prayer for Ndu, Ndi-Ichie and the kingmakers.

"Those below your level shall be loyal to you."

"*Iseee!* [Amen]" shouted those he was praying for.

"You will succeed in all you do."

"*Iseee!*"

"You will always be in good health."

"*Iseee!*"

"You shall live to see your great grand-children."

"*Iseee!*"

"Your old age will never constitute problem to your loved ones."

"*Iseee!*"

"Rise."

Ndu and his colleagues raised up their heads; all the other people in the arena raised up their heads too.

"I am convinced that God has answered all the prayers uttered by Isi-Ichie," said the master of ceremony.

As the Isi-Ichie was being led to his seat, the master of ceremony began to tell the people about the position. He said: "Isi- Ichie is the highest authority in this kingdom. Ascension to this office is by divine appointment. Wealth and fame cannot make anyone the Isi-Ichie. God is all that one needs to become the Isi-Ichie. To be the isi-Ichie, one must have to be the oldest man in this kingdom."

Isi-Ichie halted and muttered something to Ndu, when they got closer to the seat reserved for the nonagenarian. Ndu looked round and gave sign to the master of ceremony who rushed and gave the microphone to Ndu. The regent brought the microphone close to Isi-Ichie's lips; and the latter began to pray for all the indigenes and guests in the arena; as they bowed their heads.

"You will not die young," Prayed the Isi-Ichie.

"*Iseee!* [Amen]" responded the people.

"God shall hunt down all those that seek to terminate your lives."

"*Iseee!*"

"You shall not preside over the burial of your younger ones."

"*Iseee!*"

"No one shall rub you of your daily bread."

"*Iseee!*"

"After taking care of your children, your children will also take good care of you in your old age."

"*Iseee!*"

"Sit down."

The people applauded the Isi-Ichie for some time before sitting down, as directed by the old man. As the Isi-Ichie sat on the seat reserved for him, Ndu, the kingmakers and Ndi-Ichie turned and went back to their seats.

The master of ceremony continued with his narration. "As I was saying earlier … Isi-Ichie is the highest authority in this kingdom. His decision cannot be tampered with, as far as this town is concerned. He's the one that crowns the king. He can equally call the king to order, or even suspend him if the king goes against the custom and tradition of the kingdom; and if the people desire that the king should be removed. Above all, he appears and speaks in the open once in a while."

Ndu was seated next to Isi-ichie; he was explaining something to the latter while the master of ceremony kept the people busy with his tale. "This event is grand," said the master of ceremony. "We are still expecting the state governor and the honourable minister of state for culture and tourism."

Siren blared in a distance. The people paid attention to the entrance to the royal arcade. Deep inside, they believed they knew whom the siren would lead into the arena. Some believed that the state governor was the one coming, while others thought that the honourable minister of state for culture and tourism was the one coming with the siren blaring vehicle; but they all goofed. A convoy of two vehicles came into the arcade and stopped at the middle of the arena. One of the two vehicles was a jeep while the other was a Rolls Royce. On seeing the vehicles, those that knew the owner hissed and paid no further attention to the siren blaring convoy; but those that didn't know Obi Nwako before, kept staring until he came out from the Rolls Royce. Two armed policemen came down from the jeep, rushed and stood beside him.

The indigenes of Ogiga kingdom shouted, "*Heeey!*" in shock, while the *ozo* title holders stood aghast and stared at Obi Nwako who clad in *ozo* regalia.

"Chief Okoro, what is the meaning of this?" asked Ndu.

"My regent, I don't understand what you're talking about," said Okoro.

Members of the *ozo* society left to meet with Obi Nwako; leaving only the duo of Ndu and Okoro in the pavilion.

"Why is your friend dressed in *ozo* regalia? Is he a member of the *ozo* society?"

"My regent, I think Obi Nwako is the only one that can provide answers to those questions," Okoro fired back.

At that juncture, the *ozo* title holders that went to meet with Obi Nwako had gotten closer to him.

"Obi Nwako, why are you dressed like this?" asked Agbakpo.

"Chief Agbakpo, I wish you came down to my level," said Obi Nwako.

"Are you now an *ozo* title holder that you dressed like one?" asked Agbakpo.

Obi Nwako pretended not to know what Agbakpo was talking about. "Is anything wrong with my dressing? I mean, I dressed for the occasion."

"Obi Nwako, you are dressed in complete *ozo* regalia; and your name is not in our register. What you have done is sacrilegious … and it attracts austere sanctions," said Agbakpo.

"I have no problem with whatever punishment you people might decide to inflict on me. I'm equal to the task," boasted Obi Nwako."

"Obi Nwako, depart from this arena now!" Agbakpo commanded.

"Your wish is my command, Chief Agbakpo," said Obi Nwako.

As Agbakpo panted and fumed, Obi Nwako turned and entered his car.

"You will hear from us," said Agbakpo.

"I will be waiting," responded Obi Nwako.

The two armed policemen rushed into the jeep; thereafter, the convoy left the arena as siren wailed from the jeep.

"Nonsense!" said Agbakpo who instantly looked up, brooded for a while, heaved a sigh and said to the other *ozo* title holders, "Let's go back to our seats."

They all turned and went back to their seats wondering what emboldened Obi Nwako to do what he did.

Ozo was a highly respected society in Ogiga kingdom and in every Igbo community. It was a gathering of the high and the mighty ... who were forthright. This was because they adjudicated on matters. *Ozo* title holders never lied, lest they joined their ancestors without notice. Moreover, it was their responsibility to see that the custom and tradition of the people were not contravened. Becoming a member of the *ozo* society was capital intensive, hence, commoners were not seen amongst them. Before one could be initiated into the *ozo* society, such a person must have a wife, a befitting home; he must be without blemish and must have reasonable source or sources of income.

The law of the kingdom forbade non *ozo* title holders from dressing in *ozo* regalia. The law further stipulated that any non *ozo* title holder that dressed in *ozo* regalia must be compelled to join the *ozo* society. Becoming a member of *ozo* society was capital intensive, hence, non *ozo* title holders tried as much as they could, to be on the right side of the law that forbade non *ozo* title holders from dressing in *ozo* regalia.

Though Okoro was happy, he marveled at the level of courage displayed by Obi Nwako, at the royal arcade, when members of the *ozo* society confronted him for appearing in public, in complete *ozo* regalia. That incident made his respect for Obi Nwako to soar to a high level. His joy was intense. When the event ended, he abandoned his wife at the venue and went straight to Obi Nwako's house to cheer him.

Obi Nwako was in his study when Okoro arrived; his wife asked the visitor to tarry a while that her husband would join him in a jiffy.

"No problem," said Okoro.

Immediately he sat in the sitting room, his friend's wife placed a bottle of champagne and a glass before him; thereafter, she excused herself and left for the kitchen.

 As Okoro quaffed the wine served him by his friend's wife, his own wife was busy searching for him at the royal arcade. The woman got confused when almost all the people at the arena left and she didn't see her husband. When she called him on the phone; he told her that he went to see someone in relation to a particular contract he was pursuing ... and he asked her to go home that he wouldn't mind bitter leaf soup and *garri* for dinner.

When Obi Nwako came into the sitting room to see Okoro, the latter rose and began to call him, "Your royal highness."

They greeted like titled men and embraced each other.

"That was a wise one," said Okoro.

"We should be grateful to God for everything," said Obi Nwako.

"You now hold them by the jugular."

"I make money twisting and manipulating people's brains," said Obi Nwako. "I have never failed in any adventure."

"You've hit them below the belt," said Okoro.

"Are you sure they wouldn't play some pranks?" asked Obi Nwako.

"Come rain or shine, you must be initiated into the *ozo* society."

"Chief, I love what you just said. I think I have to get a glass and join you."

"You're free to do that," said Okoro.

Obi Nwako went to his bar and picked a glass. He raised the glass up after he had poured some champagne into it.

"What are we toasting to?" he asked.

"To your ascension to the throne," said Okoro.

"*Iseee!*" [Amen] shouted Obi Nwako, with joy.

They clinked their glasses and quaffed the contents of those glasses. Obi Nwako looked round to make sure no one was within hearing distance. Thereafter, he dragged Okoro to a corner in his sitting room and whispered something to him.

Okoro was so pleased with what he heard; hence, his joy increased and he embraced Obi Nwako instantly.

Members of the *ozo* society, in Ogiga kingdom gathered for a meeting at Ndu's house. That was on the first *eke* market day that came after the last *ofala* festival of late *Igwe* Okaaomee. *Eke* is one of the four days that make up a week in Igbo calendar. The meeting was convened to discuss Obi Nwako's contravention and transgression of the laws of the land; as it pertained to the *ozo* society, their insignia and every other thing that related to the prestigious group. Ndu's abode was the venue for the meeting because he was also the head of the *ozo* society. In fact, it was on the premise of being the head of the *ozo* society that he became the president of the council of kingmakers and also the regent of Ogiga kingdom. Their custom stipulated that whoever emerged as leader of the *ozo* society would automatically be the regent and also the president of the council of kingmakers. Ascending to the headship of the *ozo* society was insulated to democratic tenets; rather, it was based on the members' dates of initiation into the prestigious group. In other words, their rule stated that one would be the head of the *ozo* society if he was initiated into the society before the other surviving members of the noble group got initiated into the group; and every member of the *ozo* society was an automatic member of the council of kingmakers.

During the meeting of the *ozo* society which was convened to discuss Obi Nwako's offence, the members found themselves between two unfavourable options; and they must choose one of the options. The divergent views expressed by the members of the *ozo* society on the matter, aligned them into two different camps, depending on each member's line of argument. The meeting was full of intrigues, arguments and counter arguments. Some of the members of the *ozo* society were of the view that since there was customarily stipulated sanction, for any non *ozo* title holder that appeared in public, in *ozo* regalia ... that they should sanction Obi Nwako accordingly. Okoro gave this group all the support they needed.

There was a law in Ogiga kingdom that stipulated that any non-ozo title holder that appeared in public in ozo regalia shall be liable to punishment. Such punishment must include payment for ... and performance of all induction ceremonies that every intending member of the *ozo* society was required to perform. After which the offender would become a member of the prestigious ozo society. Okoro supported those canvassing for the above stated punishment to be inflicted on Obi Nwako, because that would make it easier for Obi Nwako to become a member of the prestigious ozo society; whether his kinsmen or his mother's people supported his desire or not.

The other group of members of the *ozo* society, vehemently opposed the call for the enforcement of the law that stipulated that any non-*ozo* title holder, that wore *ozo* regalia in public, would be made to pay and undergo initiation which would make the said person a member of the prestigious *ozo* society. This group believed that Obi Nwako intentionally breached the custom so as to arm-twist them into having him initiated into the *ozo* society. They pointed to the fact that Obi Nwako's initial application to join the *ozo* society was rejected, because his kinsmen said he was not qualified; and more so, his kinsmen claimed that his source of wealth was questionable and that he was under-aged.

It was a ding-dong thing. The members of the *ozo* society almost spent the whole day, arguing in the meeting without agreeing on the punishment that should be inflicted on Obi Nwako, for appearing in publc in *ozo* regalia. The meeting stretched into twilight; and it was almost dark when Ndu stood up and addressed his colleagues.

"We are standing between two undesirable alternatives. If we agree to accept Obi Nwako, it means that we should ignore his kinsmen's objection and thereby breach part of the customary requirements for admitting somebody into this noble association. And if we fail to accept him, then we will be setting a dangerous precedence. The question now is: What do we do?"

Agbakpo stood up and told Ndu that he sensed desperation in Obi Nwako's action. He went further to state that Obi Nwako wanted to run faster than his shadow. "To put an end to inordinate ambition that is now fermenting in our young men, and to stop rascals like Obi Nwako from taking all of us for a ride ...we should not induct Obi Nwako into this prestigious *ozo* society."

After Agbakpo was done speaking, Oji stood up and made it categorically clear that he never liked Obi Nwako. The statement irked some of his colleagues, and as they murmured, he went on to say, "In order not to set a dangerous precedence, I think we should induct and watch him closely; and punish him whenever he derails from the rules guiding members of this prestigious society."

"The responsibilities on the shoulders of every ozo title holder, is enough weight that can deter anyone from deviant behaviour," said Ndu. "Let's induct and monitor him," he concluded.

Before the meeting of the *ozo* title holders ended, they resolved to accept Obi Nwako into their fold, if he could pay the amount prescribed by their custom as restitution for his offence; and also foot the bill for all that would be done to have him initiated into the *ozo* society. This resolution gladdened Okoro's heart. He was visibly happy; and he wished it could be possible for him to fly to Obi Nwako's house that moment and break the news to him.

The news that deliberations at the meeting of the ozo title holders ended in his favour, made Obi Nwako's heart swell with joy. He thanked Okoro, the harbinger of the news for the efforts he made ... which was why the members of the *ozo* society agreed to accept him as one of them. They drank champagne and thereafter, Obi Nwako asked his friend the things he would be expected to do prior to his initiation into the prestigious *ozo* society. His friend told him all he was expected to do before he could be initiated into the *ozo* society; he went on to advise him to meet the secretary of the *ozo* society and officially collect a schedule that contained all he would do and all the money he should pay. He equally told him that the schedule would help him to know what the money he would pay will be used for.

In accordance with Okoro's advice, Obi Nwako went to see the secretary of the *ozo* society, a day after his friend brought him news that members of the *ozo* society, had resolved to accept him in their fold, if he could part with whatever amount they would want him to pay. The secretary of the *ozo* society gave him a document that contained list of all the money he was expected to pay, and what he was paying them for. He equally collected from the secretary, the bank details for the *ozo* society; and from there he went straight to the bank and paid into the account all the money he was supposed to pay.

Obi Nwako went back to the secretary's house two hours after he left that same place for the bank. The secretary was surprised when he showed him the cash deposit slip for the money he paid into the *ozo* society's bank account. Without wasting time, he requested for application form.

"Why are you going about this as if you're under pressure?" asked the secretary.

"I have to be fast about everything that concerns my initiation into the *ozo* society, lest you people have a change of mind," said Obi Nwako.

The secretary laughed before giving him the form; which he happily received ... thanked the secretary and then left with joy.

The prospective member of the *ozo* society returned his application form to the secretary a week after he collected same. The secretary noticed some omissions in the form while he went through it. More so the head of Obi Nwako's kindred did not append their signatures to the form, likewise the oldest man in his mother's family. When the secretary asked him why those people didn't endorse the form, he told him that he didn't know. He went on to tell the secretary that he spent six days begging them to sign the form and they refused to budge.

"Hence I decided to return the form without their signatures."

"Okay," said the secretary. "I will present your matter to the whole house when next we gather. I will keep you posted of whatever we decide."

"That will be very much appreciated," said Obi Nwako. "I think I have to go, so that you will have time to do some other things." he added.

"That's all right."

Obi Nwako thanked the secretary for granting him audience, thereafter, he begged to leave.

Emergency meeting of the *ozo* title holders was convened to discuss omissions in Obi Nwako's application form. All the members of the *ozo* society attended the meeting, in which some members led by Okoro suggested that they disregard the omissions, and go ahead and initiate the applicant into the prestigious *ozo* society. But the majority insisted that nothing should be swept under the carpet; and that the applicant must go and get his kinsmen and his mother's family's endorsements before he could be admitted into the association. They averred that since an *ozo* title holder was not supposed to lie or support evil, that Obi Nwako must go and get the endorsements required before he could be initiated. Also, they opined that a man's kinsmen and his mother's people were the only ones that can give a better attestation of him.

The atmosphere was tensed; the argument was a heated one. Ndu stood up and told them that he had tried to intervene in the matter between Obi Nwako and his kinsmen; and in what was between him and his mother's people. While his colleagues focused their gaze on his lips, Ndu breathed out heavily and told them that Obi Nwako's kinsmen vowed never to endorse his application for membership of the *ozo* society. They said that their reason was that they didn't know how he made his money. Concluding, Ndu told his colleagues that Obi Nwako's kinsmen claimed to be afraid of doing anything that would bring curse upon them. Hence, they decided to withhold their support from his desire to become a member of the *ozo* society. The regent went further to tell his audience that Obi Nwako's mother's family informed him that the applicant did not take good care of his mother when she was alive; and that their sister's spirit would not be happy with them, if they should by any means support Obi Nwako to become a member of the prestigious *ozo* society.

When Ndu finished speaking, some of the members of the *ozo* society suggested that the form should be returned back to Obi Nwako, and that he should be told to return the form back to the secretary of the *ozo* society, whenever he settled whatever was between him and his people.

Ndu hailed his colleagues for their stand, but not without reminding them that Obi Nwako's issue was like the proverbial tsetse fly, that chose to berth on the scrotum. He suggested that a waiver should be giving to the applicant. Ndu's suggestion was a tough one for the ozo title holders, but somehow, they reluctantly agreed to over-look the omissions in Obi Nwako's application form and have him initiated into the prestigious *ozo* society. Before the meeting was brought to a close, Ndu directed the secretary to officially notify Obi

Nwako of their resolution and also liaise with him, to fix a date for them to visit and inspect his home.

Everything about the *ozo* society was associated with nobility. The custom stated that anyone applying for membership of the *ozo* society, must have a befitting house and he must be living with his wife. Some men that were separated with their wives often went and brought back their wives when they applied for initiation into the prestigious *ozo* society. Many of those women went back to their father's houses after the *ozo* initiation rites and the ceremony that followed. Most of those women that went to stand by their ex-husbands for initiation into the *ozo* society never did that out of love, but for personal interest. The wives of the *ozo* title holders have their own group; and they were highly revered amongst women. Some men whose marriages had been officially dissolved, married new wives that stood by them during their initiation into the *ozo* society.

Moreso, to maintain the nobility that hung around the *ozo* society, intending members were made to deposit into a special account, money that would be used for their funeral when they died. They put that law in place so as to make sure that no member of the *ozo* society was buried like a commoner ... should his children not be well to do at the time of his death. Also, the special account insulated the offspring of the *ozo* title holders, from stress and financial difficulties when their fathers died. Membership of the *ozo* society in Ogiga kingdom was not open to all; it was specifically created for men of means.

The day the members of the *ozo* society visited his house was one of the happiest days in Obi Nwako's life. The purpose of the visit was for the *ozo* title holders to find out if Obi Nwako had a befitting home or not. Their host and his wife were happy to host them, because it was a thing of pride and honour in Ogiga kingdom for *ozo* title holders to set their feet in someone's home. The couple hosted the *ozo* title holders in a manner that no one had ever done before in the history of Ogiga kingdom. There was sumptuous food and drinks for everyone. Obi Nwako and his wife equally invited their friends and neighbours to the party. Even those that never loved Obi Nwako's family equally came to partake in the feast. They all ate to their fill, and many people took some food home too.

After merrymaking, members of the *ozo* society certified Obi Nwako's house as being befitting for a member of the *ozo* society. They gave him kudos and asked him to choose a date for his initiation, and communicate same to them through their secretary. Obi Nwako became ecstatic the moment they asked him to choose a date for his initiation into the *ozo* society. He almost prostrated when he was thanking the "august visitors" and at that instance he told them the day he would want to be initiated into the prestigious *ozo* society. The leadership of the society checked their programme and told him that the date chosen by him was okay by them. Before they left, they asked him to officially write and inform their secretary of the date he chose for his initiation into the noble group.

CHAPTER FOUR

When the date for Obi Nwako's initiation into the *ozo* society finally came, he and his wife woke up early, to make sure that their aides and the event planner did their works perfectly well. Their compound, the surroundings and the canopies were beautifully decorated for the event. Actually, celebration started on the eve of the initiation day. People kept vigil in the compound merrying and chatting. Obi Nwako was so anxious to become a member of the *ozo* society; though he had little time to sleep after the vigil on the eve of the initiation day, he still woke up several times to check the time. In his estimation, the day was taking long to dawn.

People thronged his compound at about fifteen minutes before noon. *Ozo* title holders and their wives were seated in the separate canopies decorated and reserved for them; while all the other groups, celebrant's friends and well-wishers sat in the various canopies provided for them. All that came to Obi Nwako's compound that day were not fortunate to find seats that they could sit on, because the crowd was much. Those that came late stood behind canopies and at different corners of the compound.

Despite the fact that it was a thing of pride and honour for any kindred to have their son initiated into the prestigious *ozo* society, Obi Nwako's kinsmen did not show up in his compound that day, likewise his mother's people. The day was very bright; the people attributed the brightness of the day to diligence shown by Onye-Ukwu, the rain maker hired by Obi Nwako. He hired the rain maker and paid him handsomely to prevent the rain from falling on that day, because it was sacrilegious for the rain to beat the *ozo* title holders while they performed initiation rites for a prospective member. It was regarded as a sign of bad omen, whenever rain fell while a new member was being initiated into the *ozo* society; the initiation rites were often suspended, whenever the rain fell during the initiation of new members into the *ozo* society. Prospective members were penalised for the rain that fell during or while they were about to be initiated into the *ozo* society. Hence, those that had intention of joining the *ozo* society were always upright in whatever they did, so as to avoid disgrace whenever they presented themselves for initiation into the prestigious *ozo* society.

At noon, Ndu stood up and told the other members of the *ozo* society that it was time they did the needful. Initiating Obi Nwako into the *ozo* society was the needful that the regent was talking about. All the *ozo* title holders stood up and picked their individual staff. The cloud became thicker the moment members of the *ozo* society came out from their canopy. Obi Nwako and Okoro looked up to the sky.

The prospective member of the *ozo* society became apprehensive, but a worriedly looking Okoro signaled him to calm down that he would take care of the situation. Other persons in Obi Nwako's compound became worried too, because the unexpected was about to happen. All eyes looked up to the sky; Okoro hastily moved to the backyard while Ndu beckoned on Obi Nwako to step out from where he was seated.

Onye-ukwu, the rain maker was seated on the ground in Obi Nwako's backyard. Beside him was a pile of stones; smoke was billowing out from the opening at the middle of the stones. From a bottle that was placed beside him, he intermittently sipped gin and spat same into the air. He heard footsteps while he made incantations, when he turned, he saw Okoro worriedly coming toward him.

"What troubles thou, Chief Okoro?"

"What sort of question was that, Onye-ukwu? Can you not see the cloud?"

Onye-ukwu looked up to the sky and smiled. Looking unconcerned, he boasted and assured Okoro that rain would not fall in any part of Ogiga kingdom that day.

"Í have not commanded the rain to fall; hence, it will not fall no matter what the cloud does."

"Those claims of yours should better be true because if rain falls, this initiation will be suspended."

"Chief Okoro, you speak as if you don't know that I'm the greatest rain maker around here."

"What I'm telling you is that if rain falls, it means that God doesn't want Obi Nwako to be an *ozo* title holder."

"I'm not a stranger. I know that," said Onye-ukwu.

"That's all right," Okoro said, and left.

When Okoro returned to the front of Obi Nwako's house, he saw him [Obi Nwako] and his wife standing at a corner with members of the *ozo* society; while guests and well-wishers watched with bated breath. The leadership of the *ozo* society wanted to perform the initiation rites as fast as they could so that the rains wouldn't meet them. Ndu told Obi Nwako that he would call him thrice ... that he should remain mute if he called him for the first and second times.

"You will only answer, when I call you for the third time. And that response of yours will automatically make you an *ozo* title holder."

Obi Nwako nodded and happily said: "Your wish is my command, sir."

Ndu cleared his throat and called him, "*Ozo* Obi Nwako," but he didn't respond.

Again, Ndu called him, "*Ozo onye di nma n'azu?*"

Expectedly, Obi Nwako kept mum. Ndu cleared his throat again and called him for the third time, "*Ozo Omelu k'okwulu.*" *Omelu k'okwulu* was the name chosen by Obi Nwako for his *ozo* title.

Nature instantly answered, before Obi Nwako could open his mouth to answer to the name. There was crash of thunder, flash of lightening, gust of wind and downpour. All of these happened almost at the same time; and to everyone's consternation.

The wind lifted Okoro and hit him against a wall; it equally blew off the caps that were on the heads of the *ozo* title holders. Also, it blew away the hired plastic chairs and canopies. Those that had gathered to witness the initiation rites ran for cover.

"Ba-d omen," said Ndu.

"*Alu,*" said Oji. [*Alu* means sacrilege]

"Abomination," Agbakpo added.

"This is sacrilegious," Ndu said again.

The *ozo* title holders picked their caps and staff; and as they were leaving, Obi Nwako and his wife stood aghast and watched them. Obi Nwako looked pitiful; he put his two hands on his head as tears began to stream down from his eyes. While the rain fell unabatedly, Onye-ukwu, the rain maker sneaked out of Obi Nwako's compound and ran home.

Obi Nwako visited Okoro in the hospital, where the latter was receiving treatment, for what happened to him during his friend's aborted initiation into the prestigious ozo society. Okoro was in the ward with his wife when his friend visited. His head and his right hand were bandaged; and he asked his wife to help him sit up the moment Obi Nwako stepped into the ward.

"How are you doing today?" asked Obi Nwako.

"I feel better," was Okoro's response.

Okoro's wife greeted Obi Nwako and excused herself. "I will be outside," she said to her husband and stepped out of the ward.

"I thank God; you look brighter today," said Obi Nwako.

"You look worried," said Okoro. "I hope all is well?" he further asked.

Obi Nwako told him that all was not supposed to be well when he [Okoro], was still in the hospital and with his dreams and aspirations shattered.

"Chief, is it still possible for me to be initiated into the ozo society?"

Okoro told him that rain marred his planned initiation, and that it was sacrilegious for rain to fall during someone's initiation into the *ozo* society.

"No other person can speak on your fate except Isi-Ichie and the chief priest of the gods. And they cannot speak until at least three months after the sacrilegious event."

The last piece of information from Okoro was like a bombshell to the one he was talking to. Obi Nwako was instantly enveloped by some degree of discomfiture due to hopelessness which Okoro's last information had conferred on him. His being disconcerted notwithstanding, Okoro went on to tell him that what should be bothering him ought to be the fast approaching election into the town union executive. "Tenure of the present executive expires in the next four months."

"How is that supposed to bother me?" asked Obi Nwako. "At least, you know quite well that I'm not vying for any position in the town union executive," he asserted.

Okoro giggled and told him that he knew he was not vying for any position in the town union executive. "But the outcome of that election will influence the nomination of whoever becomes our next *igwe*."

"Chief, I'm still lost," said Obi Nwako.

"You and I are from the same village ... I'm I right?"

"You're right, chief."

Okoro told him that Aghanya, one of the contenders for the office of the president general of the town union was from the same village with both of them. He went on to tell Obi Nwako that he would never be *igwe* if Aghanya should be elected as the president general of their town union because the constitution of their town stated that the king and the town union president general must not come from the same village. This information from Okoro made Obi Nwako's temperature go haywire. He felt cold in the inside, and at the same time, sweat was all over his body even though the temperature in the ward was not above twenty degrees centigrade. Slowly, he looked away, put his left thumb between his lips and began to imagine Aghanya as the newest obstacle to his dream of ascending the throne.

Ndu paid Agbakpo a visit two days after Okoro was discharged from the hospital; two of them had a brainstorming session over a bottle of wine. Both men were highly revered *ozo* title holders. How to solve the myriad of problems bedeviling their town was the focal point of their discussion.

"I went to see Chief Okoro, yesterday," said Ndu.

"How is he doing?" asked Agbakpo.

"He feels better now. He's been discharged," answered Ndu.

"What happened that day will show people like Okoro that God still exist ... and that he still frowns at evil," said Agbakpo.

"Hmm, I really thank God he did not die. Otherwise, the story would have been different," said Ndu.

In a lighter mood, Agbakpo told his visitor that what happened that day was like a scene in a movie. "The way the wind lifted Okoro and crashed his head and his hand against a wall was unprecedented."

"But in spite of what happened," said Ndu, "they are yet to learn their lessons."

"How do you mean?" asked Agbakpo.

Ndu told Agbakpo that Okoro and Obi Nwako were working against Aghanya's election, as the president general of their town union, despite the fact that Aghanya hailed from the same village with them. He further accused the duo of throwing their weight behind another candidate from a different village, who was equally seeking election into the same office that their brother was vying for. Agbakpo was surprised to hear that Okoro and Obi Nwako were working against their brother, Aghanya. "But why would they do such a thing?" he asked.

"I wouldn't know," said Ndu. But after a deep thought, he said that he felt the duo didn't want Aghanya to ruin Obi Nwako's chances of becoming the *igwe* of their town. "You know the *igwe* and the president general must not come from the same village. Okoro and Obi Nwako still believe that there is definitely going to be a miracle that will make the latter the king of Ogiga kingdom."

"Tall dream," said Agbakpo.

"Mere rhetoric cannot stop them," said Ndu. "The council of kingmakers must have to take affirmative action," he added.

"What do we do then?" asked Agbakpo.

Ndu wanted to provide an answer to Agbakpo's question, but the alarm on his phone beeped and interrupted him. He looked at the phone and at his wrist watch; and heaved a sigh. "I have to run now, lest I be late for an appointment," he said and rose from the seat he sat on. "We shall see later, to strategise."

"No problem," responded Agbakpo, who instantly stood up. "For as long as we are in this town, we shall never allow rascals to take over the town," he concluded.

Ndu nodded, smiled and said: "I share your view, Chief Agbakpo."

Agbakpo walked his visitor to his car, and after they had given each other parting handshake, the regent entered his car and drove off, while Agbakpo went back … into his house.

Agbakpo could not sleep at night; he stayed awake all through the night wondering what Okoro and Obi Nwako had up their sleeves, that they were hell-bent on destroying the custom and tradition of their town. His greatest worry was why both men failed to mind what the possible repercussion of their actions might be on two of them, their families and the entire kingdom.

Obi Nwako paid Okoro a visit to intimate him of his meeting with Ezenwa, one of the contenders for the office of the president general of Ogiga town union. Prior to his friend's arrival, Okoro was watching television in his sitting room; plaster was still on his fore-head … one of his hands was supported by bandage that hung on his neck. He was happy when his visitor told him that Ezenwa appreciated the support both of them were giving to him despite his archrival, Aghanya being an indigene of the village both of them came from.

"I pledged to support him with ten million naira."

"That's good," said Okoro, "but what we should do is this…"

Obi Nwako stared and patiently waited for Okoro to complete his last statement, but the latter was not in a haste to do that. He took some time to think over the suggestion he wanted to make. When he was done thinking, he breathed out heavily and said: "We will give him five million naira for his campaign; while we use the remaining five million naira to bribe the delegates that will vote in the election. By this, we will leave no room for shortcomings."

To Okoro's consternation, Obi Nwako rose from his seat and began to pace about. After some time, he halted and brooded for a while; later on, he nodded and smiled. "*Chei!*" he exclaimed. "Chief, you're a genius. Do you know I never thought of it that way?"

Okoro smiled and told him that any child that stayed close to elders had the propensity to learn a lot.

"Chief, you're wise."

"I always thank God who endued me with wisdom," Okoro said and grinned.

Obi Nwako stared at his host admiringly for some time and shrugged; thereafter, he assured him that he would do as he had suggested. Okoro was delighted when Obi Nwako agreed that they would give five million naira to Ezenwa and then use the other five million naira to buy over the delegates that would vote in the election and mandate them to vote for Ezenwa.

"Ezenwa will automatically win the election if you do as you just said," said Okoro. "And that will pave the way for you to become our next *igwe*," he concluded.

All the other members of the council of kingmakers met with Aghanya in Ndu's residence, at exactly the same time Okoro and Obi Nwako, were meeting in Okoro's house. During the meeting in Ndu's house, the regent assured Aghanya that all the kingmakers were behind him. He went on to tell him that Okoro and Obi Nwako that came from the same village with him, abandoned him and chose to support Ezenwa, because of some sinister motives of the duo. Furthermore, Ndu promised Aghanya that all of them in that meeting would make sure that all the delegates from their villages, cast their votes for him.

"I've also been in contact with branch leaders of our town union within and outside the country. They all promised that their delegates will vote for you."

Aghanya was elated by what Ndu said. He prostrated and thanked the kingmakers. "Thank you my regent," said Aghanya. "Thank you my chiefs," he added."

The kingmakers smiled; Ndu asked Aghanya to stand up. Aghanya stood up; filled with joy, he told them he didn't know what to say or how to thank them.

"I'm short of words," he said. "Thank you all for finding me worthy of your trust. On my honour, I promise never to dash the confidence you repose in me."

Twenty-four hours after the list of delegates that would vote in the town union election was released, Okoro came to Obi Nwako's house panting and fuming. That was many weeks after the former was discharged from the hospital. Obi Nwako was seated at the balcony when his visitor arrived; he was surprised by the mood his visitor was in. Nevertheless, he greeted and offered him seat. Okoro thanked him and sat on one of the seats at the balcony.

"Is everything all right?" asked Obi Nwako.

"Members of the council of kingmakers are the obstacles we must have to surmount now, if we must not fail in making Ezenwa the president general of our town union."

"How do you mean?" asked Obi Nwako."

Okoro giggled and answered, "The delegates rejected the money we offered them to vote Ezenwa in as our town union president general."

"Why did they reject the money?" asked Obi Nwako.

"All the other members of the council of kingmakers used their position to sway the delegates' support to Aghanya."

Obi Nwako went into deep thought; thereafter, he said: "In that case, Ezenwa is going to be returned unopposed on the day of the election."

Okoro was surprised by Obi Nwako's boasting. He wondered why his friend thought it would be possible to make Aghanya drop his ambition ... for Ezenwa to be the president general of their town union.

"I hope you've not forgotten that Aghanya is more popular," said Okoro.

"Don't worry about that," replied Obi Nwako.

"You really think it will be possible to convince Aghanya to shelve his ambition?" asked Okoro.

"You worry too much chief. I will suggest you leave that to me."

Okoro pouted and stared at him; he equally gave Okoro a weird look before he looked away and smiled. Okoro then hummed and shrugged; he later wondered the magic wand his friend would use to make Aghanya drop his ambition.

In less than seventy-two hours after Obi Nwako boasted that Ezenwa would be returned unopposed during the town union election, a gang of three men abducted Aghanya on his way home. He was driving home after meeting with some prominent indigenes of Ogiga kingdom that came back from Europe and America for the town union election, when a van coming from the opposite direction blocked his way. He was alone in his car while three young men were seated in the van.

Aghanya was stunned, he watched with mouth agape as two of the three occupants of the van came down with guns. The armed men got to his car, opened the door and dragged him out. They pushed him into the van; and sandwiched him in the back seat. They left Aghanya's car at the middle of the road and drove off with him.

Car horn honked at the front of Ndu's compound. The gateman rushed and peeped to see who was at the gate; his master came out from the house with a newspaper while he was opening the gate for the visitor. As Ndu stood at the porch with a newspaper in his hand, he focused his attention at the gate to know who the gateman was opening the gate for. Agbakpo drove into the compound while the gateman held the gate open. The gateman closed and locked the gate immediately Agbakpo's car screeched into the compound. The visitor parked his car and alighted from it with worries written all over his face. Ndu stood inert and watched Agbakpo with rapt attention as he matched closer to him.

"You look worried. I hope all is well?"

"My regent, there is fire on the mountain."

"Sit down," said Ndu.

Agbakpo thanked his host and sat on one of the seats at the porch. Ndu observed him for a while before sitting down; thereafter, he asked: "What happened? You look ruffled."

"Aghanya is missing," said Agbakpo.

"What!" Ndu exclaimed.

Ndu was so surprised, hence, he didn't know the particular question to ask Agbakpo. "How ...? Where ...? When ...?"

He asked all these questions in quick succession without waiting for his visitor to provide answer to any of them.

"Pull yourself together, my regent."

Ndu managed to pull himself together, thereafter, Agbakpo went on to tell him that Aghanya's car was found at the middle of Ama-iyi road two days earlier. "No one has seen him since then," Agbakpo concluded.

"Incredible," said Ndu. "Nothing like that has ever happened in this town before."

"It baffles me too," said Agbakpo.

"How much are his kidnappers demanding as ransom?"

Agbakpo told Ndu that all efforts to establish contact with Aghanya's kidnappers proved abortive and that no one knew whether he was still alive or not. Ndu shrugged and told Agbakpo that they needed to do something quickly; but Agbakpo told him that he was confused and bereft of ideas. On a second thought he asked: "What do you suggest we do?"

Ndu brooded for a while and suggested that they got Isi-Ichie acquainted first. The idea pleased Agbakpo, and he suggested that they matched words with action immediately.

"Let's go," said Ndu.

Both men rose from their seats and hastily moved to where Agbakpo's car was parked. While Agbakpo was unlocking the car's door, Ndu asked the gateman to open the gate for them. As the gateman unlocked and held the gate open; the two men entered Agbakpo's car and drove out of the compound. The gateman closed and locked the gate immediately the car left the compound. As they navigated their way to Isi-Ichie's compound, Ndu brought out his phone ... called some of their colleagues, and requested that they joined him and Agbakpo, at Isi-Ichie's compound immediately that something unprecedented had happened.

Isi-Ichie's compound was empty when Ndu and Agbakpo arrived and parked. Isi-Ichie's son came out from the house while they alighted from the car. The youmg man greeted the duo of Ndu and Agbakpo; upon inquiry, he informed the visitors that his father was having lunch. Ndu asked him to tell his father that they came to see him. He asked the two chiefs to sit down while he took their message to his father. Both men sat down at the porch while Isi-Ichie's son went into the house. He returned after a short while and informed the visitors that his father would be with them in a jiffy. Ndu thanked him for his effort, thereafter, he excused himself and retired back into the house.

While Ndu and Agbakpo were chatting and waiting for Isi-Ichie to come out, Oji, Afoka, Iloka, Okeke, Okoro and Uka arrived in quick succession. The newcomers exchanged greetings with Ndu and Agbakpo and sought to know why they were summoned to Isi-Ichie's compound. Ndu wanted to answer the newcomers' question, but Isi-Ichie showed up, Instead providing the needed answer to the question, he rose with Agbakpo ... and together with their other colleagues they bowed down to show reverence to the most respected man in Ogiga kingdom.

Isi-Ichie was surprised to see the chiefs that were gathered in his compound without notice. He acknowledged their show of reverence to him; then he went on to ask: "I hope peace has not departed from this kingdom?"

"*Nna anyi* [elderly one], if we don't do something urgently, peace may bid farewell to this kingdom soon," said Ndu.

Isi-Ichie looked up and brooded for a while; then he asked his visitors to sit down. They complied with the directive; Isi-Ichie sat down too expecting them to tell him why they came to see him, but none of them said anything. He waited for some time ... and broke the silence.

"What is the matter?" he asked.

"Aghanya is missing," answered Ndu.

"How do you mean?" asked Isi-Ichie.

Ndu nudged Agbakpo to tell Isi-Ichie what happened.

Agbakpo informed Isi-Ichie that Aghanya was last seen two days previous to the day they were having that discussion. He went further to say that Aghanya was last seen in a meeting, with delegates from Europe and America that came home to vote, in their town union election that was forthcoming. Agbakpo told Isi-Ichie that no one had seen or heard from Aghanya since he left the venue of that meeting for his house. While the nonagenarian was wondering if Aghanya could have embarked on an emergency travel without informing anyone, Agbakpo shocked him by letting him know that Aghanya's car was found abandoned at the middle of Ama-Iyi road.

When Agbakpo finished telling Isi-Ichie all he knew about Aghanya's disappearance, Ndu said that the spirit was telling him that Aghanya's kidnap was not for ransom or ritual purposes. "I strongly believe it has to do with the town union election which holds at noon tomorrow."

They kept mum and looked at each other when Ndu finished speaking. After some time, Isi-Ichie hummed, shook his head, appreciated his visitors' fears and went on to tell them that Aghanya's kidnap was the first of such incident in their town since he was born. He appealed for calm and promised that perpetrators of that crime would not go scot-free. He equally assured them that nothing would happen to Aghanya, the kidnap victim. "I will order the youth to search every nook and cranny of this town for our kidnapped brother."

Okoro's countenance showed that he was not happy with the action Isi-Ichie wanted to initiate, but his colleagues happily believed that the nonagenarian was in order. Isi-Ichie asked Ndu and Agbakpo to call the youth's leader and the outgoing president general of their town union for him, thereafter, he asked the others to go home.

"Does anyone have any other thing to add?"

His visitors remained mute and looked at each other. Isi-Ichie raised up his hand and said: "May peace be unto you all."

"Iseee!" shouted his visitors who then lowered their heads and chorused: "May you live long, *nna anyi.*"

Isi-Ichie rose from his seat and waited … it was until his visitors departed that he went back into his house.

Though it was already dusk, from Isi-Ichie's compound, Okoro went straight to Obi Nwako's house, to intimate him of the action the Isi-Ichie had resolved to take … so as to have Aghanya rescued from his abductors' den. On hearing that the youth would be mobilized to comb through the whole town in search of Aghanya, Obi Nwako became apprehensive. He snapped his fingers and muttered: "This is serious."

Okoro watched as his friend stood up and began to pace about in his sitting room.

"Hey!" Obi Nwako exclaimed as he brought out his mobile phone from his pocket. He made call to the leader of the three-man gang that kidnapped Aghanya, and instructed him to move their captive to another town at dawn, because the youth of Ogiga would be combing through everywhere in search of their captive. He equally ordered them not to move that night because the town's vigilante group often mounted road-blocks at night. "Be careful," he said to the gang leader, "and leave no traces," he added and ended the call.

"I pray they succeed," said Okoro.

The following morning, the three abductors came into the room that they kept Aghanya in and tied his eyes with black cloth; they equally tied his two hands together and hurriedly led him out of the room. When they brought him out of the house, they pushed him into their van; thereafter, they rushed into the van and sped off. The van was approaching the boundary between Ogiga and a neighbouring town on top speed. Aghanya whose hands and eyes were still bound was sandwiched in the van's back seat by two of his abductors; while the gang leader was behind the wheel.

As the van negotiated a bend, the abductors sighted a police checkpoint that was manned by four armed policemen. A police van was parked close to the checkpoint. The gang leader stamped his foot on the brake pedal; and decided to attempt a U-turn on the narrow road. As the abductors' van was struggling to do a U-turn on the narrow road, the policemen rushed into their van and sped toward the abductors.

The policemen's latest action made the gang leader to change his mind. He engaged the reverse gear and wanted to escape with the vehicle moving backward; but the police van got closer to them before they could go far on reverse. The abductors van stopped abruptly, the three-man gang abandoned Aghanya in their van and attempted to escape, but luck ran out on them ... they were all shot dead by the policemen.

After the policemen had inspected the dead bodies of the three abductors, they went to their [abductors'] van and saw Aghanya shivering in the van. When they brought him out from the van, he pleaded with them not to kill him that he would give them any amount of money they wanted. The policemen untied his hands and eyes, and asked him to relax that nobody was going to kill him. His mind experienced respite when the men told him that they were policemen.

The policemen searched the abductors' van, after that, they threw the dead bodies into the back panel of the van used by the criminals for their evil operations. Two policemen entered the abductors' van while the other two policemen entered the police patrol van with Aghanya. The policeman on the driver's seat of the abductors' van turned on the ignition and moved. The siren in the police vehicle wailed as it followed the abductors' van. Furthermore, the blue light on the roof of the police vehicle flashed as the siren wailed.

CHAPTER FIVE

There was tension and palpable fear in Ogiga, following the sudden disappearance of Aghanya, who was a top contender for the position of president general of their town union. All the concerned indigenes of the town believed that his abduction had something to do with his desire to be the town's president general. Because of that, prominent persons in the town gathered in Isi-Ichie's compound to chat the way forward for their town.

Those in the meeting included Isi-Ichie, all the ozo title holders, other members of the council of kingmakers, Ndi-Ichie and the outgoing executive of their town union etcetera. Almost everyone in the meeting opted for the suspension of the town union election which was to hold that day, but Okoro opposed the idea vehemently; and asked them what they would cite as their reason for suspending the election.

"We are to give them the obvious reason," said Agbakpo. "We will cite the present security breach in our town," he concluded.

"I support the move for the suspension of the election until we get to the bottom of this matter; and reinvigorate our security architecture," said Ndu.

"The election cannot be suspended," said a voice; from the gate.

They all turned to see who the intruder was. Lo and behold, they could not believe their sight when they saw Aghanya approaching them with the four armed policemen that rescued him. They were dazed, while Isi-Ichie remained seated all the others stood up and stared ... as Aghanya and the policemen moved closer to them.

"I am alive," said Aghanya. "The election must hold."

All those that were standing ... sat down the moment Aghanya prostrated before Isi-Ichie.

"Rise my son, nothing will happen to you," said Isi-Ichie.

Aghanya got up as directed by Isi-Ichie and told them how he was abducted by a three-man gang. He equally informed them that his abductors wanted to take him to their hideout in a neighbouring town; and that the police later killed all the gang members and set him free. All the people in that meeting except Okoro were happy that Aghanya made it back alive. They thanked the policemen for a job well done, but the officers asked them not to worry that they merely did their job.

Ndu looked at his time piece and screamed, "The election is in twenty-five minutes' time."

Others looked at their wrist watches and corroborated Ndu's claim.

"Let's rush to the election venue immediately," said Ndu.

All the ozo title holders, the other members of the council of kingmakers and the members of the outgoing town union executive etcetera hastened out ... leaving Isi-ichie and Ndi-Ichie in the compound. Ndi-Ichie was a group of old men of which none was below eighty years, and it was from amongst them that the Isi-Ichie emerged.

Community primary school Ogiga was thronged by indigenes of the town. They gathered there because of the town union election that was to be conducted that day in the school premises. The people's mood was ambivalent. Because of Aghanya's disappearance, the indigenes of Ogiga kingdom didn't know whether they still needed the town union election or not. They stood in small groups discussing with each other. Some of them opined that it was because of the election that Aghanya was abducted; they went on to assert that the election ought to be suspended indefinitely, until Aghanya was found. Another group of people at the venue believed that it was not wise for the election to be suspended because of one man's predicament; they wondered why anyone should suggest that their town should remain standstill just because one man was kidnapped by some folks.

Obi Nwako and Ezenwa were at the venue too, and they were complacent about Aghanya's disappearance, because they thought that the issue would make the election a mere work over for Ezenwa. They started celebrating with their supporters at about five minutes to the time slated for the commencement of the election; but their celebration was truncated almost immediately.

They heard some noise outside the school premises; but they didn't bother themselves about that, until the noise got closer and louder. It was then that they turned and focused their gaze at the gate, with the intention of seeing some hired thugs coming in to cause some problems at the election venue; but they were surprised when they saw those making the noise. Obi Nwako thought he had seen a ghost when he saw Aghanya being led into the school premises by Ndu and the other chiefs. The weather was very cold that day, but Ezenwa began to sweat profusely because he knew the game was over, the moment he saw Aghanya coming into the election venue with the chiefs. When Aghanya and the horde that came with him got closer to where Obi Nwako was standing with Ezenwa, Okoro left the crowd and went to his friends.

He told his friends that Aghanya appeared as they were meeting in Isi-Ichie's compound ... and informed them that the police killed his abductors and rescued him. Obi Nwako was devastated by the narration given by Okoro. Looking confused, he shouted in agony ... tears welled up in Ezenwa's eyes. Aghanya's sympathisers and supporters began to rejoice the moment they saw him. Their celebration was more like a victory party, though the election was not yet conducted.

Delegates to the election balloted immediately accreditation was concluded. At the end of the process, the votes were sorted and counted, and as expected, Aghanya was declared winner. Like every election loser, Ezenwa was not happy with the outcome of the election, but Obi Nwako was pained much more than Ezenwa that contested the election with Aghanya.

Obi Nwako felt that his world had crashed since Aghanya, who hailed from the same village with him had been elected president general of their town union. Okoro tried very hard to console him but Obi Nwako was shattered beyond redemption. The trio of Obi Nwako, Okoro and Ezenwa left the venue angrily the moment they saw Aghanya and his supporters dancing and celebrating their victory.

Obi Nwako's wife was seated in the sitting room watching television when her husband tottered in with Okoro and Ezenwa. She greeted and welcomed them before attempting to leave ... but her husband asked her to get them a bottle of gin and three glasses from the bar that was located in the extended part of the sitting room. The three men sat down with their mournful faces while the woman went to bring the bottle of gin and three glasses. When she brought the bottle of gin and three glasses, she poured some gin in the three glasses and served them before departing for the kitchen.

Obi Nwako mumbled while they quaffed many a glass of the gin. He later opened up and told his friends what was disturbing him. He told them that some of his friends were *igwe* in their respective towns, and that their journeys to the thrones of their ancestors were not as turbulent as his desire to rule over his people.

"All hope is not lost," said Okoro. "We can still remove Aghanya from office via impeachment."

"How possible can that be?" asked Obi Nwako. "I hope you've not forgotten that the only person we have in the town union executive is the vice president general?"

"Just believe," said Okoro. "There's nothing impossible under the sun. Hold on to your dream. No retreat."

"No surrender," responded Obi Nwako.

Ezenwa remained indifferent while Okoro tried to convince Obi Nwako that all hope was not lost, and that they could still remove Aghanya from office through impeachment. A lot of things were going on in his [Ezenwa's] mind then. He was counting the opportunities and pecuniary gains he lost by losing the election to Aghanya. Unknown to many that were either sponsoring or supporting him, he wanted to be the president general of their town union so that he would use the office as cover to indulge in clandestine businesses with the government, contractors, and oil companies that operated in their town.

Some weeks after the town union election was conducted, Ndu requested that a meeting of the members of the council of kingmakers be convened in Isi-Ichie's compound. Unlike other meetings convened by Ndu, this one was not to discuss issues pertaining to the development of their town; but the meeting was to tell his colleagues and Isi-Ichie that his life was in danger. Quite unlike him, he remained visibly apprehensive all through the meeting which took place in Isi-Ichie's compound.

"A group of fully armed young men barged into my house recently and ordered me to amend our constitution, within one month or resign; if I still love my wife and my life."

"And what is the spirit telling you?" asked Oji.

"I want to step down," answered Ndu.

Okoro was elated when Ndu stated that he wanted to step down from the positions he held in their town, but the other chiefs in the meeting kicked against Ndu's planned resignation … and assured him that nothing would happen to him.

"Regent," Agbakpo called, "if you chicken out, who else do you think will step into the shoes you will abandon?

"You're a retired commissioner of police, regent. You can provide for yourself any kind of security that you might need," said Oji.

"In all honesty, I can provide for myself any kind of security that I need. But, what about my loved ones? What about my friends and relatives?"

"Regent, we all agreed never to let this great town of ours slide into the hands of charlatans," said Uka. "We must fight on."

"No retreat," said Agbakpo.

Okoro kept sealed lips, but all the other chiefs chorused: "No surrender."

Isi-Ichie told Ndu that it was not by mistake that the almighty God chose him to be the head of the ozo society and subsequently the regent of their great town. He further told him that God chose him for the positions he held in their town, because God knew he could perfectly discharge the responsibilities associated with those positions creditably and responsibly, based on his contacts and experiences. Before the meeting was brought to an end, some of the chiefs advised Ndu to call off the armed men's bluff that they won't do him anything, while some others suggested that he should get police escort that would be following him about, until the tension in Ogiga kingdom died down.

Ndu went with his wife to see his in-laws on a Sunday afternoon. As they were coming back, Boss began to follow them immediately they left his in-law's house. Half way into their journey, he said to his wife, "It's like we're being followed."

"How do you mean?"

"The car behind us has been following us since we left your father's house."

His wife turned to see the car that had been following them; Boss sped up, over took and blocked them. Ndu pressed his car's brake pedal hard with his foot, this made his car to come to an abrupt halt. While he stared at Boss and his car, he wondered why a young man like him could be driving recklessly.

Boss came out from his car and moved straight to Ndu's car. As Ndu and his wife stared with mouths open, Boss opened the door to Ndu's car and shot him severally; thereafter, he went back to his car. While the regent's wife fidgeted, he entered his car and sped off. The woman waited until Boss' car had gone out of sight before she shook and called her husband severally; but the man did not answer. She became worried and confused; tears began to stream down from her eyes. She cried for a while before pulling herself together; later, she made calls to Aghanya and Agbakpo and informed them that her husband had been shot by a gunman. She told them the location and equally requested for help, so that her husband would be taken to the hospital for medical attention.

Ndu's wife was pacing up and down by her husband's car crying; when Aghanya arrived with youth leader. The woman told them what happened, and as they were trying to transfer Ndu's body to Aghanya's car, Agbakpo and Uka got to the scene; and lent the duo of Aghanya and youth's leader some help. They later asked the woman to sit by her husband's body in Aghanya's car. Also youth leader was asked to follow Aghanya's car with Ndu's car. Aghanya entered his car and drove off; youth leader followed him immediately with Ndu's car. Agbakpo and Uka entered the former's car and followed them.

While they were taking Ndu to the hospital, Uka called some *ozo* title holders on the phone and informed them that there was an attempt on Ndu's life; and that they were taking him to the hospital.

The three vehicles came into the hospital in the same order that they left the scene of the crime; and parked at the hospital's car port. Youth's leader came down from Ndu's car and rushed into the reception. After a short while, youth leader came out from the reception ... two stretcher-bearers were following him with a stretcher.

They brought Ndu out from Aghanya's car and put him on the stretcher. As they were carrying him into the hospital ward, Okoro and some other members of the *ozo* society arrived the hospital; and sought to know what happened; how, when and where it happened. Aghanya coughed and told Okoro and those that came with him all that the victim's wife told him when he got to the scene of the incident with youth leader.

In the hospital ward, the medical doctor on duty checked and confirmed Ndu dead. His wife found it difficult to believe what she heard ... in her confused state, she held the doctor and besought him to do something and bring her husband back to life. The doctor gently freed himself from her grip and left the ward. Ndu's wife fell to the ground instantly and cried uncontrollably. A nurse covered Ndu's body with a cloth ... tears welled up in the eyes of all the men in the ward, except Okoro.

"Hey! ... Sacrilege!" exclaimed Aghanya.

"*Chei!*" Uka shouted; and went on to say: "Darkness has befallen our land."

Agbakpo shook his head and said: "We must get to the root cause of this."

Okoro was unsettled by Agbakpo's last statement. He panted, gave Agbakpo a weird look and shook his head. Despite the fact that every indigene of Ogiga that was in the hospital that day cried because of Ndu's death, Okoro didn't blink his eyes.

In fact, he was happy but he tried very hard to conceal the joy that filled his heart.

Isi-Ichie was devastated when the news of Ndu's demise got to him. "The regent was immutable. He was truthful, peaceful and honest. And he believed in justice," said the Isi-Ichie.

After saying lofty things about the slain regent, the nonagenarian told those around him that the murder of their regent had pushed the truth farther away from their town. He refused to eat for days, thereafter, he laid terrible curse on those that hatched and perpetrated the evil act. Ndu's death shook the entire town. Both the young and the old; indigenes and strangers wept when the news of his demise got to them.

While the whole town was in a mournful mood following Ndu's assassination, Okoro and Obi Nwako were rather unconcerned. The duo converged at a garden in Obi Nwako's compound and gulped wine and chicken to celebrate the death of the man they saw as obstacle to their aspirations.

"Now that you're the regent," said Obi Nwako, "I hope our plans will sail through without any hiccup."

"You can say that again. Though I've not been officially named the regent, but, in no long time, you'll become the *igwe* [king]. That's definite."

"I trust you," said Obi Nwako. "And I know what you can do."

They were still celebrating Ndu's sudden demise when the two armed policemen that were always around Obi Nwako came and informed him that they've been ordered to report back at their station with immediate effect.

"What nonsense are you people talking about?" asked obi Nwako. "Excuse me," he said to Okoro; therafter, he picked his phone and called the Divisional Police Officer (DPO) in charge of Ogiga police station. He became confused when the DPO told him that the order to recall the two policemen attached to him came from above. He ended the call abruptly and went into a deep thought.

"Is anything the matter?" asked Okoro.

"No ... No problem at all," answered Obi Nwako.

Obi Nwako heaved a sigh; then he gave some money to the policemen and asked Amadi to drop them off with the jeep. The two policemen boarded the jeep and the driver drove off immediately.

Obi Nwako and Okoro were still seated in the former's garden strategising on how to get their town under their feet when Amadi came back. Shortly after the driver came back, a car pulled up at Obi Nwako's gate. As Amadi was going to the garden to tell his boss that he was back, four armed policemen stormed the compound in a manner reminiscence of commandos. At gun point, the law enforcement officers asked everyone in the compound to remain still. Obi Nwako got infuriated.

"Gentlemen, what is the meaning of this?" he asked.

One of the policemen sized him up and said: "You are under arrest for the murder of Chief Ndu Onyechi."

Okoro was surprised; also, the gateman and the two drivers in Obi Nwako's employ were shocked by what the policeman said.

"Youngman," said Obi Nwako, to the policeman, "I hope you realise the gravity of the allegation you just levelled against us?"

The policeman sternly warned Obi Nwako to remain silent, because whatever he said might be used against him in the court of law. He then asked them to move … Okoro expected Obi Nwako to call the state commissioner of police who was his friend, but Obi Nwako did not do that, hence, he reminded him of the need for him to do that.

Obi Nwako asked him to relax that there was no cause for alarm. The duo started moving toward Obi Nwako's car …

"And where are you going?" asked the policeman.

"To the car," said Obi Nwako … Or, are we going to trek?"

"Our vehicle is outside," said the policeman.

Obi Nwako looked at the policeman disdainfully; but that notwithstanding, the policeman insisted that the two suspects must follow them in the police vehicle.

As Okoro and Obi Nwako headed to the gate, the policemen asked John and Amadi to join them.

"We are just drivers," cried John.

"Come on move!" shouted the policeman.

The policemen led the four suspects out of the compound and ushered them into the police vehicle that was parked outside the compound; and zoomed off with them … leaving the gateman behind. The quartet spent some days in detention; … and were later released, because the police lacked credible evidence with which to prosecute them.

Days after Okoro and the other people suspected to have hand in the killing of Ndu were released by the police, a meeting was convened in Isi-Ichie's compound to fill the vacancy created by Ndu's death. The meeting which was chaired by Isi-Ichie was attended by all the Ndi-Ichie and all the members of the council of kingmakers which comprised of all the *ozo* title holders and elected representatives of all the villages in Ogiga kingdom.

During the meeting, Okoro was officially made the regent and pro tempore *igwe* of Ogiga kingdom. While making his acceptance speech, Okoro thanked the people for the confidence reposed in him and for standing by him while in detention. He went on to acknowledge the fact that Ndu's death was a very big loss to their town; and the feet chosen to wear the big shoes left behind by the deceased were too small. Nevertheless, he promised to do his best, and never to let them down. Before he concluded his acceptance speech, he told them that he was accepting the responsibility given him with a proviso. As his listeners adjusted their sitting positions and paid much attention to him, he said: "Based on the precarious security situation in our land, I can only sit on the throne for a period not exceeding four months."

Everyone in the meeting was stunned by Okoro's proposition; hence, they pleaded with him to remain on the throne as their pro tempore *igwe* [king] for a period not less than eight months, but he refused; and he rather enjoined the members of the council of kingmakers to go back to their respective villages and convince people to step forward for nomination as *igwe* ... and he equally stated that they must do that within four months.

Okoro's stand almost caused problem in the meeting, but isi-Ichie in his wisdom ruled that they would not force someone to be a pro tempore *igwe,* for a period longer than the time the person's spirit allowed him to act as their king. He went on to implore the kingmakers to work harder and nominate someone that could be made the king of Ogiga kingdom before the expiration of the deadline given them by Okoro. Isi-Ichie's resolution gladdened Okoro's heart, and as he celebrated, the other chiefs looked at each other in amazement.

Two weeks after Okoro's installation as regent, he summoned the kingmakers to a meeting in his house. During the meeting, he sought to know the number of persons from their respective villages that showed interest in becoming their *igwe.* He was surprised that many minutes after he requested the list of those seeking nomination as *igwe* that no one gave him even the name of a person that was interested in the throne.

"No names?" he asked.

Iloka told Okoro that the security situation in their town had instilled fear in those qualified to come forward for nomination as *igwe.* He equally said: "The stringent conditions in our kingship constitution have prevented rugged and courageous young men that can standup to the situation from coming forward."

"So what's the way out? What do we do?" asked Okoro.

Oji suggested that they should have their kingship constitution amended so that younger, influential and rich sons of their town would be eligible to vie for the exalted position in their town. "And who knows, if we throw the door widely open, we may get someone that may be able to arrest the crime situation in our town."

Okoro's body language prevented those that attended the meeting from making quality contributions or air their views during the meeting. Okoro had been an advocate of the amendment of their kingship constitution. Prior to his emergence as the regent of their town, he lobbied for an amendment to the constitution, so as to pave way for Obi Nwako to become the king of Ogiga kingdom. Because of that, no one opposed the request for the amendment of their kingship constitution. Docility of Okoro's colleagues made him ecstatic. His colleagues remained mute when he sought to know if anyone was opposing the motion for the amendment of their kingship constitution. "Can we now, go for the amendment of the kingship constitution?"

Agbakpo adjusted his sitting position, cleared his throat and told them that he would support the amendment if it would be with a proviso. "If the amendment can only be tenable for the selection of the next *igwe*, then I will support it," he concluded.

Agbakpo's assertion pleased his colleagues and they nodded in agreement. After Agbakpo had ended his speech, Okoro nodded for some time and slid into a deep thought which lasted for awhile; then he spoke in support of Agbakpo's stand. The meeting ended with the resolution that the Ogiga kingship constitution should be amended as quickly and as possible. Okoro's joy knew no bound that day because the meeting went the way he wanted it to. He was highly elated to the extent that after the kingmakers had gone, he celebrated the resolution made at the meeting of the council of kingmakers with the members of his family.

After the meeting of the council of kingmakers which was the first to be held in his house, Okoro asked Obi Nwako to choose a date for his coronation and start sending invitation cards to his friends and associates. Obi Nwako appeared lost; he sought clarification; Okoro told him that the battle had been won; that members of the council of kingmakers had resolved to amend their town's kingship constitution, so that people like Obi Nwako could be nominated as *igwe*. An elated Obi Nwako thanked Okoro for his doggedness, and promised to surprise him immediately he was crowned the *igwe* of Ogiga kingdom. He equally informed Okoro that the two policemen that were withdrawn from his house had been deployed back.

CHAPTER SIX

A forthnight after Okoro's installation as the regent and the pro tempore *igwe* of Ogiga kingdom, Aghanya came back from a journey, and was having lunch with his wife ... someone banged on their door. The couple looked at each other; they focused their gaze at the door as the frequency and intensity of the bang increased.

"Who could that be?" muttered Aghanya.

"Let me find out," his wife responded, and went to the door.

As she unlocked and opened the door, the leader of a four man armed police team pushed her backward; she fell on one of the seats in their sitting room. Four armed policemen rushed into the sitting room and pointed their guns at the couple.

Aghanya was irked; he stood up and berated the team leader for pushing his wife in his presence and in his house. He later scolded the entire team severely for unprofessional conduct, thereafter, he went on to ask them what gave them the effrontery to barge into his house the way they did.

"Shut up, Chief Aghanya," ordered the team leader. "We are here to arrest you for armed robbery."

Aghanya and his wife were shocked when the policeman said they came to arrest him for armed robbery.

"I can see that your brain has taken flight from your skull," said Aghanya. "What was that statement supposed to mean?" he sternly asked the policeman.

The team leader told him that it would pay him a lot if he could remain silent as whatever he said might be used against him in the court of law. Thereafter, he asked one of his men to arrest Aghanya. The policeman that was asked to arrest Aghanya went closer and wanted to handcuff the suspect, but Aghanya resisted.

"If you don't respect yourself Chief Aghanya," the team leader said while removing his gun from safety, "I will blow off your head right away; and nothing will happen."

Aghanya's wife became jittery the moment the policeman threatened to shoot her husband.

"I know it's either there is a mix up somewhere or this might be a clear case of mistaken identity," she said.

Aghanya looked at her.

"Sweetie, please comply with them," she pleaded.

Aghanya's heart melted … because of his wife's plea; he surrendered his hands to the policeman and he was instantly handcuffed.

As the policemen were leading him out of the house, he turned and said to his wife, "Call Barrister Ikpeama immediately."

"Okay dear," responded his wife.

The policemen pushed him out of the house. His wife looked worried and confused as she watched the policemen leave their compound with her husband. She later pulled herself together … brought out her mobile phone and made a call to

Barrister Ikpeama; and informed him that her husband was taken away by a team of policemen. The barrister promised to go to the police station immediately and find out what the problem was. She ended the call and heaved a sigh. After she had cleared the table, she picked her car key and dashed out of the house.

Agbakpo was driving out of his compound while his gateman watched. Police vehicle blocked his car immediately his car entered the road. He would have hit the police vehicle if not that he swerved his car sharply before applying the brakes. He came down from his car looking furious ... the four armed policemen that arrested Aghanya came down from the police vehicle with their rifles, leaving the handcuffed Aghanya alone in the vehicle.

"My friend what sort of driving was that?" Agbakpo asked the driver of the police vehicle. "Didn't you see that a vehicle was coming out from the compound?"

"We are sorry for the dangerous driving Chief Agbakpo. But we are here to arrest you for armed robbery," said the leader of the police team.

Agbakpo's gateman was shocked when the policeman said that they came to arrest his boss for armed robbery.

Agbakpo got infuriated and told the team leader that he could sense that his father didn't raise him up properly; and neither did those that employed and armed him give him proper training

"Will you take this your rickety vehicle out of my way before I lose it," Agbakpo ordered the police team leader.

"Get him!" the team leader ordered a junior officer.

"Get who?" asked Agbakpo. "You must be out of your mind," he further said, and began to move to his car.

All the policemen pointed their rifles at him, he halted out of fear. The team leader removed his gun from safety and said: "Take no further steps Chief Agbakpo."

Agbakpo's gateman became afraid for his boss' life; but surprisingly, his boss began to   bluff, "Shoot me! Shoot me!" he yelled at the police team leader. "What are you still waiting for? Do you think that I'm afraid of death? Come on, shoot!"

The police team leader gave sign to a junior officer. The junior officer brought out handcuffs and moved closer to Agbakpo. To everyone's consternation, when the junior officer touched Agbakpo, he saluted the junior officer with a thunderous slap and screamed: "Come on take your hand off me! Buffoon, what do you take me for?"

"We have respected you enough Chief Agbakpo," the police team leader said, with great fury and fired three shots very close to Agbakpo's feet.

Agbakpo jumped up in fear when each of the three shots was fired; he later screamed and said: "It hasn't gotten to this now. What if any of the bullets had hit me?"

"Stretch your hands now," said the team leader.

The suspect fearfully surrendered his two hands to the junior officer. Without wasting time, the junior officer handcuffed and asked him to move.

The gateman stood aghast and watched as his master was being led to the police vehicle. Agbakpo turned and asked him to call Chief Oji and Chief Okoro immediately. Before he entered the vehicle, he turned again and asked the gateman to write down the police vehicle's number.

"Yes sir," said the gateman.

Agbakpo was stunned when he bent to enter the police vehicle. That was because he saw Aghanya seated quietly in the vehicle with handcuffs.

"Chief, good afternoon, sir," greeted Aghanya.

"What is really happening?" asked Agbakpo.

"Chief, I don't know. I am as perplexed as you are," said Aghanya.

Agbakpo breathed out heavily and entered the police vehicle. The four policemen entered the vehicle too. As the vehicle zoomed off, the gateman rushed out, squatted and wrote the vehicle's number on the ground. He went into the gate house when the vehicle had gone out of sight ... later, he came out with pen and paper which he used to copy the number that he wrote on the ground. He brooded for some time before he opened his master's car ... and removed the key from the ignition. He locked the car's doors before going into the compound. As he locked the gate, he said to himself, "When madam comes back, she will drive the car into the compound."

Prominent indigenes of Ogiga town converged for a meeting in Isi-Ichie's compound. The meeting was held two days after Agbakpo and Aghanya were arrested by the police. Attendees at the meeting included the Isi-Ichie, all the members of the council kingmakers and Ndi-Ichie etcetera. The meeting was convened at Okoro's instance and the purpose of the meeting was to build confidence in the attendees; allay their fears and put their town back on the part of progress. The meeting deliberated on a lot of things that concerned their town; and before the meeting was brought to a close, Okoro implored all that attended the meeting to go back to their respective villages and plead with their people to step forward for nomination as *igwe*. He hinged his plea on the fact that Aghanya and Agbakpo who were alleged to be the kingpins of the criminal gang that was terrorising their town had been arrested by the police. All the attendees maintained sealed lips while Okoro was speaking; and after he was done with his speech. He expected reactions but no one said anything in support of … or against all that he said. After a while, Isi-Ichie spoke in support of Okoro's request. "There is nothing to be afraid of anymore," he said. "Go to your people, convince them to step forward and serve our town," the nonagenarian concluded.

Everyone in the meeting was surprised when Oji stood up and sought to know if there was proof that those arrested by the police were not "innocent of the allegation made against them." He went on to say that, "Obi Nwako framed up those suspects that are in police net."

"Chief Oji, how are you sure of that?" asked Isi-Ichie.

"Obi Nwako wrote petition to the state commissioner of police," said Oji, "and falsely accused Chief Agbakpo, Aghanya and others that are at large of robbing him of his money and other valuables."

"That's a new twist that we really need to investigate," said Isi-Ichie.

Isi-Ichie's assertion pleased everyone in the meeting, except Okoro who advised that they should be careful, so as not to arrogate to themselves the duty of the court.

"Let's wait until the court proves them guilty, or discharge and acquit them," opined Okoro.

Okoro's position did not please any of those men that were in the meeting, but none of them was courageous enough to challenge him, lest they fall victim of what they knew nothing about. Isi-Ichie understood their predicament …. Consequently, he shook his head in dismay and requested that one of them should move a motion for the meeting to be brought to an end. The motion was moved and supported. They later ended the meeting with a prayer … and that was after they've agreed to reconvene in a month's time.

When the prominent indigenes reconvened in a month's time, Okoro sought to know if any of the attendees collected any name or names of those that wanted to vie for the throne of Ogiga kingdom. The response he got was on the negative side; hence he reiterated the need for their kingship constitution to be amended so that the conditions for becoming the *igwe* would become less stringent. "Perhaps," he said, "we may get some courageous young men who will want to serve our people if we change some of the requirements."

Nobody opposed Okoro's wishes. He got all he wanted. The kingship constitution of Ogiga kingdom was amended at Okoro's behest; not purposely for the good of their town but to pave the way for his friend, Obi Nwako to emerge as the king of Ogiga kingdom.

Amendment of the kingship constitution of Ogiga kingdom made Okoro and Obi Nwako joyous, because the amendment removed the clause that stated that anyone seeking to be the *igwe* of Ogiga kingdom must be a member of the prestigious *ozo* society. But Aghanya's emergence as the president general of Ogiga town union was yet another hurdle before them, because Aghanya was from the same village with the duo, and their constitution stated that the king and the president general must not come from the same village. The duo had sleepless nights and spent a lot of money to have Aghanya impeached.

Their joy became complete the day Aghanya was impeached and his deputy who hailed from a different village sworn in as the president general of Ogiga town union. Obi Nwako celebrated Aghanya's impeachment in a great way. He threw a party to that effect and there was surplus food, drinks and gifts for those that attended the party. Aghanya and Agbakpo were still in police detention when the former was impeached. Many believed that Obi Nwako framed both men up because he saw them as the obstacles to his emergence as the king of Ogiga kingdom. While they celebrated, Okoro asked Obi Nwako to send his letter of intent to him as soon as possible. "Include in the letter the date you've chosen for your coronation, then go ahead and invite your friends and well-wishers. For it is done."

"What would I have done without you, chief?" asked Obi Nwako, who went and prostrated before his friend. "Thank you, sir," he said and remained on the floor until Okoro smiled and tapped him on the back.

People thronged the royal arcade on the day of Obi Nwako's coronation as the king of Ogiga kingdom. The occasion was grand and it was attended by isi-Ichie, Ndi-Ichie, Obi Nwako and his wife, all the members of the council of kingmakers except Agbakpo, kingmakers' wives, young and old persons, women, children, policemen, journalists, dwarfs, cultural troupes, members of the town union executive and their wives, government representatives, captains of industries and Obi Nwako's friends and well-wishers. Most of the people that graced the occasion were non indigenes of Ogiga kingdom. Many people in Ogiga did not attend the coronation ceremony because they were of the view that Obi Nwako was not qualified to rule over them; hence they chose to mind their businesses in their various homes. Those at the arcade sat on seats designated for them, and that was a month after Obi Nwako submitted his letter of intent to Okoro. The duo chose not to waste time planning for the coronation lest another obstacle resurfaced and thwart the progress they made while their kingship constitution was being amended.

The throne was placed under a canopy that was specifically designed for it. The well decorated canopy had royal insignia on it, and seated around it were members of the council of kingmakers and Ndi-Ichie. The crown was placed on a golden tray that was placed on the throne; beside the tray was the royal staff. Two dwarfs guarded the throne and all that were placed on it, while armed royal guards stood by the four metal posts that supported the canopy that provided shade to the throne.

Cultural groups invited to the occasion took turn to entertain the people that gathered at the royal arcade to witness the coronation ceremony. At noon, they were asked to stop performing; the field was cleared and people were ordered to stop moving about. The moment absolute quietness was maintained at the venue, Ndi-Ichie and the members of the council of kingmakers rose on their feet; every other person stood up too, but Isi-ichie remained seated. One of the dwarfs that guarded the throne picked the tray on which the crown was placed, the other dwarf picked the royal staff; two of them went and stood close to Isi-Ichie with the crown and the staff. Okoro beckoned on Obi Nwako to come and kneel before Isi-Ichie; Obi Nwako did that hastily ... His wife stood behind him while he knelt before Isi-Ichie.

Okoro collected the microphone from the master of ceremony and held it close to Isi-Ichie's mouth. Isi-Ichie cleared his throat and thanked those that created time out of their busy schedules, to come and witness the epoch-making event taking place in Ogiga kingdom, on that particular day. He prayed for peace and progress of their town; he went further to pray for the well-being of the indigenes of Ogiga, their tenants and others that came from different places to witness the coronation ceremony. After the prayers, he said that what they gathered at the royal arcade to do was in consonance with the custom and tradition of their town as handed over to them by their ancestors. He also prayed for the soon to be crowned king's peaceful reign and wished that his reign would bring peace, security and development to their town.

Later on, Isi-Ichie picked the crown from the golden tray held by one of the dwarfs and said: "By the authority vested in me, I hereby crown you, Obi Nwako as the ruler of Ogiga kingdom."

Thrice, he put the crown on Obi Nwako's head, and thrice did he lift the crown off his head. He then put the crown on Obi Nwako's head the fourth time and allowed it to rest thereon. The people shouted: "*Ochie-eee!*" [He has been crowned].

Okoro collected the royal staff from the other dwarf and said: "This is the staff ... the symbol of authority in this kingdom. With the power vested on me as the regent, and with the Isi-Ichie's approval ..."

Isi-Ichie nodded in agreement; Okoro continued, "I hereby hand over to you, the staff of authority. May you reign for a long time ..."

Obi Nwako received the staff; rose on his feet and raised up the staff. The people shouted: "*Igwe-eee!*" the moment he raised up the staff.

Obi Nwako's wife hugged him; fire was set to the twenty-one cannons set outside the arcade, and it fired twenty-one times. While the canons were blazing, *igba-eze* cultural group came out with their drums and provided melodious tunes which Obi Nwako, his wife, his friends and well-wishers danced to while going round the royal arcade. Before he sat on the throne, he made acceptance speech in which he promised to bring development to the kingdom and also restore peace and security to the land of their ancestors.

The police took Agbakpo and Aghanya to court a week after Obi Nwako's coronation. The duo mounted the dock when their case was called up ... they pleaded not guilty to the charges against them. Some indigenes of Ogiga kingdom were in court that day to show solidarity with the men standing trial. The accused persons were denied bail by the court and the judge ruled that the two men should be remanded in the correctional centre until the next time their case would come up in court. The case was adjourned for three months; and the police took Agbakpo and Aghanya to the correctional centre as ordered by the court.

From the court, Ikpeama, who was counsel to the two accused men, went straight to Isi-Ichie's house with the wives of the accused men, to brief the nonagenarian on the progress of the case. While they were discussing with Isi-Ichie, Oji came to see the nonagenarian. Oji was among those that did a lot of things underground to get Aghanya and Agbakpo released but to no avail.

Ikpeama informed Isi-Ichie that Agbakpo and Aghanya had no case to answer, and that they were suffering because some persons in the police high command seemed to have personal interest in the matter. Agbakpo's wife interjected the lawyer and said that, "Obi Nwako has bribed all the senior police officers; that's why they want the two innocent men dead."

Ikpeama shook his head and continued speaking, "*Nna anyi* [elderly one], we've been able to see the director of public prosecution. We made him understand that the allegation against Chiefs Agbakpo and Aghanya was a charade, a frame-up and a figment of Obi Nwako's imagination. Chief Oji was with us that day."

"That's true, *nna anyi* Isi-Ichie," said Oji. "I equally told the director of public prosecution that Agbakpo was in a meeting with me and other chiefs and elders from this town on the day and time the alleged robbery incident took place. More so, I informed him that Agbakpo lived with me after his graduation from the university; and that he got his first job while still living in my house, hence, I can vouch for him that he's not a robber."

Agbakpo's wife told Isi-Ichie that she didn't know that Obi Nwako's desperation and evil heartedness could get to the extent that he could frame-up her husband in armed robbery. "My husband never took what belonged to another person. My husband always allowed people to have their way instead of having brawl with them."

"*Nna anyi* Isi-Ichie, there's more to this issue than meet the eye," said Aghanya's wife.

"Is that so?" asked Isi-Ichie.

Aghanya's wife hissed; shook her head and said: "Anyway, I told the director of public prosecution that my husband was not in the country as at the time and day the alleged robbery incident took place. I showed him my husband's international passport and flight ticket to buttress my claim. In short, *nna anyi* [elderly one], they arrested my husband forty-five minutes after he came into town; and he was enjoying the sumptuous meal I prepared for him when the police came and took him away."

Isi-Ichie was happy because of all the things his visitors had done in trying to get Agbakpo and Aghanya out of the hook. "Maintain the pressure," he said, "leave no stone unturned until our brothers are released."

Amidst sobs, Mrs Aghanya and Mrs Agbkpo knelt and begged Isi-Ichie to use his powers to impress on Obi Nwako to withdraw his petition against their husbands. Isi-Ichie asked them to rise; sit down and wipe their eyes. They complied with the directive; Isi-Ichie went on to assure them that nothing would happen to their husbands. Furthermore, the nonagenarian called Barrister Ikpeama and said: "As far as this case is concerned, I will like you to make sure you create no opportunity that our adversaries might exploit."

As he bowed to show reverence to Isi-Ichie, Ikpeama said: "We will do nothing other than your wish, *nna anyi.*"

"May the almighty God guide, protect and see you through," Isi-Ichie prayed.

"A-men!" chorused his visitors; who equally bowed, to show respect to the Isi-Ichie.

CHAPTER SEVEN

Agbakpo and Aghanya's trial divided Ogiga kingdom into two different groups. The first group was made up of Obi Nwako, Okoro and few individuals that either fed or depended on the former's deceitful benevolence for survival; while the other group was made up of members of Agbakpo's family and members of Aghanya's family; friends of the accused men, well-wishers and other lovers of justice who resided within and outside their town but who shared the same ancestry with the two men being tried for robbery. The two groups used the three months that lay between the day the case was first called up in court and the date the case was adjourned to ... to test the veracity of their social contacts. Within the three months, members of the two groups met those they knew in government ... who they believed could be useful in making the court's judgement swing to their favour. While Obi Nwako was busy bribing some government officials that would help influence the case to his favour, members of the other group worked very hard to prove to the government officials that the accused men were innocent ... and that Obi Nwako made up the robbery story. Expectedly, activities of the two groups escalated tension in Ogiga kingdom.

When the three months elapsed, members of the two groups went to court to observe the trial of the accused men. They went early to the court so that they could get seats in the court room. Officials of the correctional centre brought

Agbakpo and Aghanya to court before the court commenced sitting. The court treated many cases that day; the one involving Agbakpo and Aghanya was called up last. When the case was called up, those that came for the case adjusted their sitting positions and listened with rapt attention. But to everyone's chagrin, the judge struck out the case, citing withdrawal of interest in the case, by the prosecution as his reason. The judge's pronouncement stirred up an uproar in the court room. The accused men became overtly ecstatic. Members of Obi Nwako's group who were led to the court that day by Okoro were stunned and upset; while members of the other group jubilated. Getting the jubilant crowd to calm down was one hell of a task for the judge and the court clerk. The judge kept pounding his gavel on the table, while the court clerk kept shouting: "Si-len-ce in court!"

When the noise subsided, the judge berated the crowd and advised that they behaved themselves in the vicinity of the court. "Í rise," he said and stood up.

"Co-urt!" shouted the court clerk.

Everybody in the court stood up and stared as the judge walked into his chamber with his police orderly. Aghanya and Agbakpo were visibly happy ... people shook hands with them and congratulated them as well. Their elated spouses hugged them and shed tears of joy while holding them; thereafter, they went out of the court room with their friends and well-wishers.

Agbakpo and Aghanya's acquittal was a very big blow to Okoro and Obi Nwako; the newly crowned king was devastated when Okoro came back from the court and informed him that the accused men had been set off the hook.

"Why? How?" he asked in quick succession ... and rose from the throne in angst.

"Prosecution withdrew interest in the case," said Okoro. "And I strongly believe that the director of public prosecution has hand in it."

"Chief Okoro, there's fire on the mountain. The presence of Chief Agbakpo and Aghanya in this kingdom means trouble. Anarchy! Hey!"

"I believe we still have a card to play," responded Okoro.

"What's the card?"

"We can petition the attorney general and commissioner for justice."

Obi Nwako was pleased by Okoro's response; he smiled and said: "Chief you're a genius. I never thought of that."

"Hold your peace and lose no sleep," said Okoro, "for we must get Agbakpo and Aghanya off the way."

"I'm now happy," Obi Nwako said and sat back on the throne. "Sit down chief, and let's get you some kola."

"We can do that when next I visit. I have to go now. My wife has been disturbing my phone with calls."

"If you insist," said Obi Nwako.

"I insist."

"That's all right. Give my regards to your wife," said Obi Nwako.

"I will," Okoro said, and headed for the door.

The moment Okoro left ... the king breathed out heavily and began to ruminate over some things. Among the things he thought about was the strategy he would adopt, so that he would not be disgraced out of his new position.

Isi-Ichie summoned prominent indigenes of Ogiga town to a meeting, about a week after the robbery charge against Agbakpo and Aghanya was quashed by the court. In the meeting, the nonagenarian told them that he solicited their presence because he desired to get to the root of the imbroglio that had bedeviled their town. "Ogiga kingdom has never had it so bad before," he said, and went on to appeal to his audience's conscience.

His speech had sobering effect on almost everyone in the meeting, but Okoro and Obi Nwako were indifferent. Isi-Ichie was still speaking when four armed policemen stormed into his compound which was the venue of the meeting. He punctuated his speech the moment he sighted the law enforcement officers. "Who are these ones?" he asked.

"They look like men of the police anti-robbery squad," said Okoro.

"What could their mission be?"

"Isi-Ichie, let's wait till they get closer," said Okoro.

They all focused their gazes on the policemen who were advancing toward them.

"Good afternoon chiefs," said the leader of the police team.

"Good afternoon," responded Oji.

"We are here to arrest Chief Agbakpo and Aghanya," said the leader of the police team.

Agbakpo and Aghanya were shocked by the assertion made by the leader of the police team; some others were surprised but Okoro and Obi Nwako were happy.

"What is their offence?" asked Oji.

"They allegedly robbed one Chief Obi Nwako," answered the leader of the police team.

"The court threw away that case last week," said Oji. "So who gave the order you came to carry out?" he went on to ask.

"The order was given by the state commissioner of police, sir," responded the leader of the police team.

"I doubt you know what you came here to do," said Oji.

The police team leader chuckled and told Oji that the state commissioner of police knew perfectly well why he and his team were in Isi-Ichie's compound to arrest Agbakpo and Aghanya. Oji became confused and wondered why the commissioner of police would order the arrest of the two men for an offence which the court had acquitted them of. While Oji was still swimming in the ocean of surprise, the police team leader ordered Agbakpo and Aghanya to stand up and follow them. The two men rose from their seats, and as the others stood up and watched in amazement, the duo followed the policemen to the police vehicle that was parked outside the compound. The policemen ushered the suspects into the vehicle first; the vehicle zoomed off after the four policemen had hopped into it.

Isi-Ichie ended the meeting abruptly, and directed Oji to get in touch with Barrister Ikpeama immediately, and inform him that the police had arrested Agbakpo and Agbanya, for the same offence the court acquitted them of. Okoro winked the eye at Obi Nwako; the latter responded; two of them stood up and happily went to where they parked their vehicles ... they left the place before every other person.

The state commissioner of police granted audience to Ikpeama, Oji, Mrs. Agbakpo and Mrs. Aghanya a day after the two men were arrested in a meeting in Isi-Ichie's compound. Their visit to the state commissioner of police office was prompted by Aghanya and Agbakpo re-arrest, for a crime which the court had said they had no case to answer. The commissioner of police told them that he did not re-arrest the suspects on his volition. When his visitors demanded to know why the two men were re-arrested for the same alleged offence which the court had ruled that they had no case to answer, the commissioner of police told them that the attorney general and commissioner for justice requested that the suspects be re-arrested.

"Why would he give such order, after court of competent jusisdiction has discharged and acquitted both men?" asked Ikpeama.

"He stated in his memo that he wants to vet their case file and make sure that the right thing was done before the case was struck out by the court," said the police commissioner.

Ikpeama wondered why the state attorney general and commissioner for justice woke up to vet a case file after the court had struck out that particular case.

The commissioner of police sympathised with Ikpeama and those that came with him. He further assured them that the attorney general and commissioner for justice must surely order for Agbakpo and Aghanya's release, if the duo were innocent. His phone rang while he was still speaking, "Excuse me," he said to his visitors, before answering the call.

His visitors waited patiently till he finished conversing with the caller. Thereafter, they sought clarifications on some other things before leaving his office.

After the meeting with the state commissioner of police, Ikpeama, Oji, Mrs. Agbakpo and Mrs. Aghanya went straight to attorney general's office; from there, they moved to Isi-Ichie's house to brief him on the outcome of the meetings they had with the two commissioners. The quartet told the nonagenarian all that the commissioner of police told them when they entered his office; they equally told the Isi-Ichie all that the commissioner of police told them after answering the telephone call that interrupted their meeting.

"Why did he re-arrest them?" asked Isi-Ichie.

"He said that the state attorney general and commissioner for justice requested the police to re-arrest Agbakpo and Aghanya," answered Oji.

"What is the attorney general's interest in the matter?" asked Isi-Ichie.

Ikpeama told Isi-Ichie that the attorney general said that Obi Nwako's counsel sent petition to his office complaining about the manner the case was struck out by the court; and that Obi Nwako later came to his office with one Chief Okoro crying foul ... and they equally told the chief law officer of the state that there was threat to lives and property in this town.

"Who is threatening who? Was he referring to our own Chief Okoro?" Isi-Ichie asked, in quick succession.

"Maybe," answered Ikpeama.

"It should be our own Chief Okoro," said Oji, "because Chief Okoro is Obi Nwako's confidant."

Isi-Ichie bent his head and brooded for a while; when he raised his head up, he asked: "So what is the attorney general planning to do with our brothers?"

Ikpeama told him that the attorney general promised to diligently study the case file, interrogate the complainants, and then come and speak with prominent sons and daughters of Ogiga kingdom, with a view to determining whether or not there was a prima facie case against Agbakpo and Aghanya.

"Let him come then. We're waiting for him," said Isi-Ichie.

Before asking the quartet to go home and rest, Isi-Ichie thanked them for the tireless effort they were making to see that Agbakpo and Aghanya, regained their freedom faster than expected. He later gave special thanks to Mrs. Aghanya and Mrs. Agbakpo for their doggedness ... and assured them that he would do everything humanly possible to make sure nothing happened to their husbands. He prayed for four of them, thereafter, the quartet bowed and departed from his presence.

With a letter in his hand, Okoro looked tensed up as he stood in his sitting room. Apparently, the letter in his hand was the cause of his worry. He began to pace about in his sitting room after ruminating over the issue that got him agitated. Intermittently, he perused the letter in his hand while pacing about … Confusion crept into his head as he paced about for a long time; at that juncture, he halted and reflected on the latest problem that demanded his urgent attention and that of his friend, Obi Nwako. His thinking expedition was punctuated by a knock on his door. He breathed out heavily and hissed; while gazing at the door. "Who is there? Come in."

Obi Nwako stepped in beaming.

"Good a thing you're here, your highness."

Obi Nwako was surprised. "Is anything the matter?" he asked.

"Please pardon my manners. Sit down first, your highness."

Obi Nwako sat down and waited patiently for his host to tell him why he was tensed.

"Chief, you haven't told me why you're worried."

Okoro hissed and shook his head. "Your highness, a big problem has just reared up in our camp."

When Obi Nwako demanded to be told in clear terms what the problem was, Okoro informed him that the attorney general and commissioner for justice wrote to inform him that he would be coming to speak with notable sons and daughters of their town, and that his intention was to find out if the allegation against Agbakpo and Aghanya was a politically motivated frame up.

Obi Nwako relaxed and asked: "Is that why you are agitated? Let him come. We will maintain our stand if he comes."

"That's not the issue, your highness."

"Then tell me what the issue is."

"Hey!" Okoro shouted, and told his visitor that their adversaries had got two witnesses that would meet with the attorney general on that day. He went further to explain to Obi Nwako that one of the witnesses was a medical doctor that claimed to have treated him in his university days after a reprisal attack on his cult group by a rival cult group left him with gunshot and stab wounds. Obi Nwako was shocked by what he heard, but Okoro was not done ... He continued, "They claimed that it was the rival cult attack that left you with the incision and the gunshot wound you claimed were inflicted on you by Agbakpo and Aghanya.

Obi Nwako snorted and looked at the part of his body where those marks were.

"But, your highness, were you a member of any secret cult when you were in the university?"

Obi Nwako was unsettled by that question; he became downcast for awhile, and then mumbled, "*Ehm* ... *ehm*, even if I was a member of a secret cult in my university days ... that's my past. Is there anyone without a past?"

"Your highness, there's another lady that is coming to testify against you; before the attorney general."

Obi Nwako got agitated and said: "I've heard enough. What we have to do now is to make sure that those witnesses never get to meet with the attorney general."

"That's the problem," said Okoro. "They concealed the identities of the witnesses, likewise the way and the manner they will meet with the attorney general."

Obi Nwako snapped the fingers and shouted: "Hey!" thereafter, he rose from his seat and rhetorically asked: "Why is fate so cruel to me?"

While Okoro stared and appeared confused; Obi Nwako cogitated for some time ... and again, he shouted, "Hey!" with the snapping of the fingers. As he paced about bemused, Okoro tried very hard to make him pull himself together. Before the duo parted on that day, they resolved to use both seen and unseen forces to make sure the attorney general's visit didn't turn in favour of Agbakpo and Aghanya.

While the people of Ogiga waited anxiously for the day the attorney general would come to their town, Okoro and Obi Nwako did all within their powers to know the identities of the witnesses lined up to speak to the state's chief law officer; but to no avail. They had believed that everyone would do their bidding once they threw some cash around, but they were proven wrong by all the people they attempted to bribe in their quest to have the attorney general's visit be in their favour.

Respite appeared to have come the way of Okoro and Obi Nwako, on the day slated for the attorney general's visit to their town. Early in the morning of that day, the attorney general called and informed Okoro that he wouldn't make it to their town, because he would be attending an emergency state executive council meeting at the same time he was supposed to be in Ogiga. He apologised for any inconvenience his absence might cause the indigenes of Ogiga, and promised to send some staff of the ministry of justice to visit in his stead and do the findings for him. Okoro was happy that the attorney general would not make it to their town as scheduled. But all through his telephone conversation with the attorney general, he concealed the joy that filled his heart, and pretended as if he wasn't happy that the legal luminary aborted his scheduled visit to Ogiga kingdom. He equally told the attorney general that they would make do with those he might send to represent him. The attorney general laughed and asked him to make sure that those that might come in his name were made comfortable. They ended their telephone conversation on a friendly note, but that was after Okoro had promised to take good care of those that would come to represent the attorney general in the meeting. After the telephone conversation, Okoro fell on his knees and thanked the almighty God for the emergency state executive council meeting … which would make it difficult for the attorney general to visit Ogiga town in person.

Royal aides asked Okoro to sit in Obi Nwako's sitting room and wait for the king whom they said was busy in his study. While waiting for his friend, Okoro kept himself busy with the bottle of wine which the royal aides served him with, and he had consumed half of the bottle's liquid content before Obi Nwako came out to see him. He rose from his seat immediately the king came out. "*Igwe-ee,*" he said.

"You are welcome, Chief Okoro. Please sit down."

"Thank you your highness," said Okoro who instantly sat back on his seat. His host equally sat on one of the seats in the sitting room.

"Your highness, God has answered our prayer."

"What happened?"

"The attorney general said he's no longer coming."

"Why?"

"He has to attend an emergency meeting of the state executive council …"

"Does that mean that he's discarded the idea of coming to interact with our people?"

"He sent some officials of the ministry of justice," said Okoro. "They are already in Isi-ichie's house."

"This is good news. Let me get my cheque book," said Obi Nwako, who hastened into his room immediately.

He came out from his room some minutes later and requested that Okoro, should accompany him to the bank, to get enough money. Upon enquiry, he told Okoro that he would use the money to subvert the officials that were sent to represent the attorney general in a meeting; which their boss was supposed to hold with notable sons and daughters of Ogiga kingdom.

Okoro was pleased with the idea; he stood up immediately and happily left for the bank with the king.

The meeting between the representatives of the attorney general and notable sons and daughters of Ogiga, ended in a way that was pleasing to the two parties that had interest in the matter under investigation. Those that believed that Aghanya and Agbakpo were innocent were hopeful that both men would regain their freedom soonest if the attorney general would work with information they gave to those that represented him in the meeting.

On the other hand, Okoro and Obi Nwako were very happy because they strongly believed that the report which the attorney general would be given, would make him see Agbakpo and Aghanya as being culpable. They were confident that both men would be indicted and awarded the maximum punishment stipulated for the offence that they were accused of. The confidence emitted by Okoro and Obi Nwako was borne out of the fact that after the meeting, they took the attorney general's representatives to Obi Nwako's house, and treated them to a royal banquet. Before the emissaries left Obi Nwako's abode, the king gave them fat envelopes that contained huge sums of money and pleaded with them to slant their report, so that Agbakpo and Aghanya would be indicted. Because of that, they believed that the emissaries had been subverted.

In the third week that followed the visit of the attorney general's representatives, Mrs. Aghanya sighted Oji while driving. Her car and Oji's car were coming from opposite directions. She flashed her car's head lamps the moment she sighted the chief. Oji responded; she honked her car's horn and pulled up. Oji pulled up too and remained in the car while Mrs. Aghanya came down from her car and rushed to meet Oji who was still seated in his car. She greeted Oji and told him that she was on her way to his house. Oji told her that he was going for a meeting; nevertheless, he managed to ask, "I hope all is well?"

"There's no new problem *nna anyi* [elderly one]. It's about the old one."

"The old one?" asked Oji. "What about it?"

She told him that it was three weeks since the officials of the justice ministry came and spoke with notable persons in their town; and with the complainants in the alleged robbery case for which her husband and Chief Agbakpo were arrested and detained. Oji nodded and verbally concurred with her.

"Since then," she said, "we have not heard from the attorney general, and my husband is still in detention with Chief Agbakpo."

Oji assured her that if the attorney general should work with the information gathered by those he sent to speak with their people that Agbakpo and Aghanya would be set free. "We just have to hold our peace. There's nothing to be afraid of."

"That's the problem, *nna anyi.*"

"How do you mean?" he asked.

"*Nna anyi*, I learnt that *Igwe* Obi Nwako bribed the officials of the justice ministry that represented the attorney general in the meeting. So ... it is obvious that they will tilt their report in favour of the king."

Oji was shocked when Aghanya's wife told him that Obi Nwako bribed the emissaries from the ministry of justice. He tapped his fingers on the steering wheel and went into a deep thought. "What are you insinuating?" he asked.

"*Nna anyi,* I suggest we see the attorney general."

"Okay. We'll see him in three days' time."

Mrs Aghanya's heart was gladdened by Oji's promise ... "Thank you *nna anyi*," she said; while genuflecting.

"You are welcome. I have to rush."

"Okay sir. God bless you, sir."

"God bless you too," he said and zoomed off, while Mrs Aghanya crossed the road ... she entered her car and sped off.

Oji lived up to his promise. He went to see the attorney general with Mrs. Agbakpo and Mrs. Aghanya three days after he made the promise. They were disappointed and almost frustrated when they got to the attorney general's office. Those they met in the office told them that the attorney general was out of town and that they didn't know anything about their boss sending a fact finding team to Ogiga kingdom. They asked Oji to come back with the two women in a week's time, if they really wanted to see the attorney general. The trio were devastated by the information they got while in the attorney general's office; but fortune smiled on them as they were dejectedly leaving the office complex. They ran into one of those sent to their town by the attorney general. Incredibly, the man put smile on their faces when they told him that they were coming from his boss' office … Reacting to what they said, the man told them that the attorney general had travelled to Abuja. As they hissed and murmured, the man advised them to go to the commissioner of police's office that the attorney general raised a memo based on their finding; and that the memo had been sent to the commissioner of police for necessary action. They thanked the man and headed for the car park, while the man climbed the flight of steps that led to his office. At the car park, Oji entered his car with the two women and zoomed off.

The commissioner of police gave Oji and the two women a rousing welcome when they got to his office. "Have you gone to the attorney general's office?" he asked, after he had offered them seats.

"Yes," answered Oji. "But we were told that he travelled to Abuja; and that he sent memo to you based on his findings. That's why we came to see you."

The commissioner of police acknowledged receipt of the attorney general's memo about an hour prior to their visit. He told them that the attorney general stated in the memo that Agbakpo and Aghanya had no case to answer. "He has directed that both men should be released immediately."

"Sir, are you serious?" asked Mrs Aghanya.

"I can't joke with something as serious as that, madam."

"Prai-se the Lord!" shouted Mrs Agbakpo.

"You people should wait in the reception. They will be released to you immediately."

They thanked the commissioner of police before walking out of his office with immeasurable joy.

True to the commissioner of police's word, Agbakpo and Aghanya were released to the trio of Oji, Mrs. Aghanya and Mrs. Agbakpo; and from the state police headquarters, they drove straight to Isi-Ichie's compound. Okoro was having discussion with Isi-Ichie when Oji arrived Isi-Ichie's compound with Mr. and Mrs. Aghanya and Chief and Mrs. Agbakpo. Isi-Ichie was very happy when he saw them, but Okoro was troubled, though he concealed it and managed to say a miserable "Welcome," to Agbakpo and Aghanya. Both men acknowledged the show of concern from Okoro despite the fact that it didn't come from the depth of his heart. The duo later expressed gratitude to Isi-Ichie and others that worked tirelessly to see that they were released. Isi-Ichie thanked the almighty God for not allowing the two innocent men to be sentenced for what they knew nothing about. He equally thanked Oji and the spouses of the two victims for their doggedness which led to Agbakpo and Aghanya's release. He went further to ask Okoro to tell Obi Nwako to make sure that what led to Aghanya and Agbakpo's detention never happened again. Okoro bowed and promised the nonagenarian that he would take his message to Obi Nwako as soon as he left his presence. But the nonagenarian was not done; he mandated Oji and Okoro to tell the town union executive, to urgently over-turn Aghanya's impeachment and reinstate him as the president general of the town union. Both men assured Isi-Ichie that they would do as he had mandated them. Then Isi-Ichie emphatically said: "Tell them they have one Igbo calendar week to reinstate Aghanya."

"Your order shall be carried out to the latter," said Okoro.

"Isi-Ichie, we shall do as you have directed," Oji assured the nonagenarian.

Isi-Ichie later released them to go, so that Agbakpo and Aghanya would go home; freshen up and then eat good home-made meal. All the visitors rose ... and before they left, they bowed to show respect to Isi-Ichie.

Obi Nwako was devastated when Okoro informed him that Aghanya and Agbakpo had been released on the orders of the attorney general; and that Isi-ichie said that he wouldn't want a repeat of what led to the arrest and detention of the two men. While the king was still trying to come to terms with the fact that Agbakpo and Aghanya were back, his friend dropped a bombshell. He told the king that Isi-Ichie had directed that Aghanya should be reinstated as the president general of

Ogiga town union. The king's blood pressure shot up immediately he heard that Aghanya would be reinstated as the town union president general; he became confused, and as Okoro watched, he began to pace about in the palace.

It is four days that make up a week in Igbo calendar. Isi-Ichie gave the town union executive one Igbo calendar week, to overturn Aghanya's impeachment and reinstate him as the president general of Ogiga town union; but surprisingly, the order was carried out within two days. Aghanya could not believe his ears when the news of his reinstatement got to him. Like every other person, he had expected Obi Nwako and his supporters to put up a fight and stop the town union executive from complying with the order for his reinstatement, which came from Isi-Ichie. Even his wife could not believe it when he told her that he had been reinstated. When she finally believed, she sang praises to the Lord; thereafter, she looked at her husband eye ball to eye ball and told him that she was proud of him.

"I'm proud of you too," responded Aghanya.

"I love you," she said.

"I love you more," he responded.

She happily jumped up and hugged him.

CHAPTER EIGHT

Uneasy calm pervaded Ogiga kingdom after the reinstatement of Aghanya as the town union president general. The uneasy calm was as a result of Obi Nwako and his cohorts' disposition toward Aghanya's reinstatement. Though they pretended not to have anything against Aghanya's return to office, but their body language proved otherwise. Within the period that the uneasy calm lasted in the town, Okoro paid a visit to the palace with a view to discussing some issues that bothered on their town's development with the king. Upon his arrival at the palace, Obi Nwako informed him that a delegation from Wise-East petroleum just left the palace; and that they wanted to commence oil exploration in their community. Okoro was surprised by that piece of information; he adjusted his sitting position and suggested that they took the company's delegation along with them to leaders of thought meeting the following day, "So that they will table their proposal before the leaders of the town."

"Why do we need to go through that lengthy and rigorous protocol?" Obi Nwako furiously asked.

"How then do you give community land to them, if you do not observe the stipulated protocol?"

"I will breach the protocol and damn the consequences. The company has no time to waste. They have paid and obtained all the necessary licenses from the federal government."

"Really?" asked Okoro.

"Yes. I have even sent one of my aides to go with them to the part of our town that they will do the exploration activities."

"*Igwe*, you are extending invitation to trouble," Okoro sternly said.

"How do you mean, Chief Okoro?"

"What you are doing is a brazen violation of the laws of this great town," said Okoro. "Giving of community land to companies is a development matter; and the laws of the land vest power over such on the town union, headed by Aghanya," Okoro concluded.

"And so what?" asked Obi Nwako.

Okoro went on to educate Obi Nwako on the criteria for releasing any land that belonged to their town to any organisation. He told him that land could only be given to an organisation if the leaders of thought were pleased with the organisation's proposal.

"If the leaders of thought are pleased with an organisation's proposal and request for land, it will mandate the town union executive to allocate land to them."

He equally asked the king if he was not there when officials of the state government came and requested for land for the building of a university in Ogiga. Okoro hit his palms on each other and said: "Count me out of any aberration to the laid down rules."

"Chief, you don't seem to understand the magnitude of fortune that comes with this ... and what we stand to lose if we let this opportunity slip by."

"I'm not against the coming of the oil company to our land. What I'm enunciating is that we should observe due process so that we can avert turbulence in the kingdom."

"Chief, has it occurred to you that the only people living large are those that deal directly or indirectly with oil companies?"

Okoro brooded for a while and said: "You're right, your highness."

Obi Nwako tried very hard to get Okoro to see reasons with him. He told Okoro that if they hand over the oil company's delegation to Aghanya and his executive, that two of them would lose the largesse that would come from the oil company. He added that if two of them could hijack the delegation and front themselves as the only appointed representatives of their people that the company would deal with their town through them. "That means, royalty will be paid through us. We will control employment quota in the company... and better still, juicy contracts will be ours."

Okoro was dazed by what he heard; he smiled and moved his tongue from the right side of his lips to the left. Obi Nwako sensed that he had shattered Okoro's defence line; hence he went on to say, "Chief that means more money for us in dollars."

Okoro was stunned; with an open mouth, he thought over all that the king had been telling him. Thereafter, he nodded and concurred with the king.

State government's request for land on which they would build university was considered and approved by Ogiga leaders of thought. After approving the proposal, the town union executive was asked to allot land conducive for a university, to the state government.

In compliance with the order from the leaders of thought, the town union executive marked out land suitable for the construction of a university, and directed the youth leader to mobilise the youth to go and clear the edges of the land, so that government surveyors would know the boundary of the said land when they would come to survey it. Youth leader mobilised the youth; with machetes in their hands they set out to the proposed site for the state university which was to be sited in Ogiga town.

From afar, they sighted Turker, Williamson, Serena and Femi surveying the land marked out for the proposed university. Turker, Williamson and Serena were Americans while Femi was of the Yoruba stock. The quartet was staff of Wise-East petroleum.

The youth stood at the entrance to the land and watched the staff of the petroleum company for some time, with a view to finding out what they were doing and who they were.

"This is the land given to the state government for the building of a university," said the youth leader. "What are whitemen doing here?" he asked.

"Maybe the state government contracted them to survey the land," said a youth.

"That cannot be. The land was approved three days ago; and we were asked to clear the four edges," said the youth leader; who went on to ask, "How could the government send people to survey a land that was not clearly demarcated."

Youth leader divided the youth into three groups. He asked one of the groups to approach the staff of the oil company from the left, while the second group was asked to approach the land grabbers from the right. When the two groups left, the youth leader and the third group remained on the same spot for about ten minutes before moving in to confront the surveying team of the Wise-East petroleum. On sighting the youth leader and his team, the oil company's staff ran for their dear lives. They ran toward the right; but they were blocked by one of the youth groups; the same thing happened when they ran toward the left. When they discovered that they could not escape, they froze, knelt down … raised up their hands and begged for their lives. They were all frightened, but Femi was frightened the most … to the extent that he almost peed his trousers.

When the youth sought to know the identity of the strangers and their mission, Williamson told them that they were staff of Wise-East petroleum, and that they were surveying the land given to their company a week earlier by "king Obi Nwako" for oil exploration. Youth leader told Williamson that the king had no power to give out community land to any organisation without consulting the stakeholders in their town. "Mr Man," Youth leader said to Williamson, "this land has been marked out for the construction of a university; and the land has been released to the state government."

"No," said Williamson, "Femi and I were part of the delegation that met with the king last week. In summary, we were issued with necessary document which has the king's seal and signature on it."

"We have rules and procedures for doing things in this town," youth leader said to Williamson; and to his cohorts he said: "Get them!"

The youth pulled the strangers up and dragged them out of the bush. Pleas from the strangers that they should use their two official vehicles parked in the bush proved abortive … the youth dragged them along like criminals.

Leaders of thought meeting was going on in Isi-Ichie's compound when the youth left their parents' houses to go and work in the land marked out for the construction of a university. Present at the meeting were: Isi-Ichie, Ndi-Ichie, *ozo* title holders, town union executive and Obi Nwako. Aghanya was telling the gathering how they took the state government's delegation to three different sites. He went on to inform them that the government delegation chose the land at Ama-ani saying that it was most suitable for the building of the proposed state university.

As he was telling them that they've sent the youth of Ogiga kingdom to go and clear the edges of the land, the youth's voices filtered into the compound … and they were chanting: "*Iwe! Iwe!! Iwe!!! …*" The song was a protest song; and it implied that anger had taking over those singing it. All the people in Isi-Ichie's compound were surprised when they heard the song; they looked toward the gate and saw the youth dragging the four staff of Wise-East petroleum into the compound. Okoro and Obi Nwako were shocked. They stood up almost immediately and looked at each other. Aghanya sat down when the youth got closer. Okoro and Obi Nwako were visibly disturbed; Youth's leader raised his hand up; the youth stopped chanting.

"My chiefs, I salute you all," the youth leader said, with a bow.

"Rise, my son," Isi-Ichie said and gave Oji a nod.

"Nwata n'acho nke ya," Oji called the youth leader.

"My chief," answered the youth leader. Nwata n'acho nke ya was Youth's leaders' real name.

"Who are these ones and where did you see them?" asked Oji.

Youth leader told them that the youth went to do some work on the land given to the state government for the building of a university; and to their greatest surprise, they saw Williamson, Tucker, Serena and Femi surveying the land. "When we confronted them, they said that the land was given to their company, Wise-East petroleum for oil exploration."

"They said that the land was given to them by who?" asked Oji.

Youth leader hit Williamson on the head and said to him, "Come on answer the question."

"Take it easy young man; lest you hurt him," Obi Nwako said to Youth leader.

"I'm sorry your highness," Youth leader said with a bow; and politely asked Williamson to answer the question.

Williamson told the leaders of thought that four of them that were arrested by Ogiga youth were staff of an American oil company called Wise-East petroleum; and that their mission in Ogiga was simple. "We came because of the abundance blessing which nature endowed your community with. We want to commence oil exploration here to the benefit of your community."

"Benefit of our community indeed," said Oji. "Is that why you strayed into our land without permission? *Ndi ocha!* [White people] *Ndi ocha!!* You people have started again."

"We didn't stray into your land without permission," said Williamson. "The king is aware of our presence in your community, and he approves of it."

Williamson's last statement shocked every indigene of Ogiga kingdom that was present in Isi-Ichie's compound that day. They all turned and looked at Obi Nwako.

"*Igwe*, you heard him," said Oji. "Did you give land to them?"

Oji's question threw Obi Nwako off balance; he appeared downcast for some time ... thereafter, he hummed, hissed and shook his head as if he was regretting something. Everybody stared at him as if he was either naked or caught stealing his neighbour's pot of soup. He buried his head in shame when he noticed that all eyes were on him. After a while, he managed to pull himself together and then requested Isi-Ichie to ask the youth and their captives to excuse them. Obi Nwako's request came as a surprise to the other people in the meeting; they looked at each other in amazement and shrugged.

"Nwata n'acho nke ya," Isi-Ichie called.

Youth leader bowed and said: "I still remain loyal, *nna-anyi* [elderly one]."

Kindly do as the king has requested," said Isi-Ichie.

Youth leader told Isi-Ichie that his wish was their command; later on, he signaled the youth ... and dragging their captives along, the youth followed their leader to the backyard.

Obi Nwako told his people that Wise-East petroleum actually came to him for land. He further stated that he informed them that allocation of land to corporate organisations was not under his purview; hence he implored them to get their proposal ready for presentation to the leaders of thought during that particular meeting that was on going on that particular day. While his audience nodded to show approval to what he told the oil company, the *igwe* went on to tell the meeting that the company's delegation agreed to what he told them and left.

Okoro clapped and gave Obi Nwako kudos for handling the delegation from Wise-East petroleum with wisdom and maturity. That sycophantic act of Okoro did not go down well with Oji; and he chided the former for the inglorious act. Okoro took offence and asked Oji never to speak to him again in the manner he did. Apparently, Okoro was trying to enthrone confusion in the meeting so as to create escape route for Obi Nwako, but Isi-Ichie was wiser than him. The nonagenarian controlled the situation despite the fact that Okoro and Oji had started having supporters. Tranquility was immediately restored back to the meeting. Isi-Ichie asked Obi Nwako to continue his tale from where he stopped.

The king told them that he later learnt that Umuanika community had given land to Wise-East petroleum, and that the company was planning to move its base to Umuanika and start drilling the oil that was in Ogiga from Umuanika. He went on to highlight that it was after considering what the people of Ogiga would lose in the areas of royalty, employment and contracts that he begged the company to come back to their town. "That was why I gave them the land. I know that what I did was wrong but I did it in our own interest, hoping to publicise it in this meeting for ratification or cancellation. That's all I have to say."

Isi-Ichie asked Obi Nwako to sit down ... he waited until the king had sat down before asking others to react to all that the king had said. No one spoke or coughed. Isi-Ichie looked at those by his left hand side and those by his right hand side and shook his head in disappointment; because he knew that it was the fear of Obi Nwako that made them not to say anything. Later, Aghanya summoned up courage and stood; as others stared, he said: "Isi-Ichie, I believe strict adherence to constitutional provisions is a panacea for crisis and hidden agenda."

Some other persons stood and made contributions on the subject after Aghanya had spoken.

"*Igwe,* a society without rules will definitely plunge into anarchy," said Okeke. "To promote peace and corporate existence of this kingdom, and give longevity to your reign, always respect the constitution of this great town," Okeke admonished the king.

"*Igwe,* you did the right thing but you did it wrongly," said Oji.

"Exactly," retorted Agbakpo. "We all want good things for our town, but that desire shouldn't be a veil for blatant abuse of laid down order," Agbakpo concluded.

When Okoro stood, he told them that it was a well-known fact that their town union president general was the one vested with the power to administer land on behalf of Ogiga people. He equally made it clear that since Aghanya was the town union president general, that allocation of land to anybody by the *igwe,* was a clear usurpation of Aghanya's responsibility.

Obi Nwako was not comfortable with what his friend was saying; his countenance notwithstanding, Okoro kept saying what he was saying ... to the surprise of every other person in the meeting. Before he collapsed his weight into his seat, he asserted, "Whether the constitution was violated or not, I want us to ponder over these questions: First, are there benefits that accrue to communities that host oil companies? Secondly, do we need that oil company on our land? That's all I have to say."

Some of the leaders of thought looked at each other, while others had private discussions.

"Chief Okoro raised valid questions," said Isi-Ichie. "Are there benefits we can get by hosting Wise-East petroleum? Do we really need them in our town?"

Aghanya told Isi-Ichie that there was no doubt that coming of Wise-East petroleum to their town would be of immense benefit to them. "We need them," he went on to say.

"In other words, you want us to leave the land for them?" asked Isi-Ichie.

"Since, oil is beneath that particular land, *nna-anyi*, let the oil company have the land," answered Aghanya.

After Aghanya had told Isi-Ichie that there was nothing wrong with the idea of giving the land to Wise-East petroleum, the latter sought to know whether anyone else was skeptical. But no one uttered a word; he thereafter ruled that the land should be given to the oil company.

"But I must warn, we will never condone violation of the constitutional ... next time," the nonagenarian concluded.

"What then do we tell the state government that wants to build university on the said land?" asked Aghanya.

Okoro told Aghanya that oil cannot be found everywhere and that university could be built on any land. "Convince the officials of the state government," he further said, "to choose any of the other two sites you showed them."

"Tell them that as at the time you showed the land to them that you didn't know that it had been given to another entity for another purpose," said Isi-Ichie.

"Leave that to me *nna-anyi*," said Aghanya. "I know what to do."

"Good. You may ask the youth to come back with the staff of the oil company," Isi-Ichie said to Aghanya.

"Yes *nna anyi*," Aghanya said with a bow before going to the backyard to convey Isi-Ichie's message to the youth of Ogiga kingdom. Immediately Aghanya left to deliver the message to the youth, Okoro and Obi Nwako raised their thumbs for each other. They were visibly happy because contrary to their imagination, Aghanya did not kick against the usurpation of his responsibility by the king.

Six months after the leaders of thought meeting, Obi Nwako requested for Okoro's presence in his palace. The invitation was honoured by the latter and they spent a lot of time talking about so many issues that bordered on the development of their town. In between their discussion, Okoro asked after Wise-East petroleum. Obi Nwako told him that Wise-East petroleum was part of the reasons he asked him to come. He began to eulogise the oil company; but unknown to him, he was getting Okoro confused with the good sounding words he was using to describe the oil company and their mode of operation. When the confusion got too much in Okoro's head, he opened his mouth and asked the *igwe* to come down to his level.

"Do you know that they have started laying foundation for their office complex?" asked Obi Nwako.

"Really?" was Okoro's response.

"Can you beat that? They even told me that their rig will go up soon."

"Your highness, we still have a very long way to go in this country. If it were our people, corruption would have held the project down for many years."

"You're right, Chief Okoro. The greatest threat to our development is 'Me, myself and I' spirit. Once we eliminate that, the sky will be our starting point in this country."

"You're perfectly right, your highness."

Obi Nwako lifted a bag that was kept beside the throne, and brought out a bundle of dollar notes from it. Okoro was stunned when the king gave the money to him and told him that it was his.

"Who asked you to give this to me, your highness?"

"It is a gift from Wise-East petroleum."

"All these for me?" asked Okoro.

"That's ten thousand dollars. They said that more is coming."

"So this is what I would have missed, if I had stupidly maintained my stand on due process?"

"Are you now saying that you no longer believe in due process?" asked Obi Nwako.

"*Igwe*, forget that rubbish," said Okoro.

Obi Nwako began to laugh ... while Okoro stashed the money in his pocket.

At lunch time, on that same day that the king gave ten thousand dollars to Okoro, the *igwe* was having lunch with his wife when one of his aides came and informed him that the youth had come to see him.

"Okay," said Obi Nwako. "Tell them I will be with them in a jiffy."

The aide bowed and said: "Your wish is my command, your highness," before rushing out to inform the youth that the king would be with them soon. Obi Nwako smiled the moment the aide left his presence, he looked at his wife and continued eating. When he finished eating, he tasted some fruits; later on, he washed down all that he had eaten with a glass of wine before he stood up and went to the sitting room. He picked a big envelope from one of the stools in the sitting room; with the envelope in his hand, he went out to see the youth of Ogiga kingdom.

When Obi Nwako came out from his house with the envelope he picked from the stool in his sitting room, he met the youth chatting with each other. On seeing him, the youth left all they were doing; surged and paid obeisance to the king. "*I-gw-e-ee!*" they shouted with a bow.

"Rise, the strength of Ogiga kingdom," said the king.

As the youth stood erect, Youth's leader said: "*Igwe,* may you reign forever."

"God bless you my dear," said Obi Nwako. "I sent for you all because I was given a message for you."

His assertion heightened the youth's desire to know why he sent for them; with mouths agape, they expectantly stared at him. Beaming, the king arrogantly stared at all the youth for some time ... "Lest I forget," he said, "how many of you have seen dollar notes before?"

The king burst out laughing when Youth leader said that he had seen dollar notes in text books and magazines.

"I've seen dollars live," said a youth. "My brother brought plenty of it when he came back from America."

"Well," said the king, "whether any of you have seen it before or not, you're all going to see it here, now."

The youth shouted and happily clapped for him.

All the youth nodded when the king mischievously asked if they still remember Wise-East petroleum.

"*Igwe,* we all remember the company," said the youth leader.

Obi Nwako gave to the youth leader the envelope he was holding, and told him that Wise-East petroleum asked the youth to share the ten thousand dollars that was in it. The message from the oil company threw the youth into wild jubilation; they exclaimed ... hugged and shook each other. Youth leader's joy knew no bound when he opened the envelope and saw dollar notes for the first time in his life.

"*Igwe,* we appreciate you for your ingenuity," said the youth leader. "We would have lost the company to Umuanika community if you didn't do what you did. *Igwe,* we are thankful, and we are very proud of you."

"You're welcome," said Obi Nwako, who then went on to beg them to make sure that every youth of Ogiga kingdom got his own share of the largesse. "Those that are not here right now, and even the ones in diaspora must not be excluded ..." the king concluded.

"Trust us, *igwe,*" said the youth leader.

"That's ali right," responded Obi Nwako.

Youth leader brought out the dollar notes from the envelope and raised them up. All the youth shouted with excessive joy when they saw the money. Obi Nwako smiled and went back into his house. Youth leader put the money back into the envelope; thereafter, the youth happily sang and marched out of the compound.

CHAPTER NINE

Operational base of Wise-East petroleum in Ogiga town [which comprised of office complex and residential quarters for their staff] was completed in so short a time. Upon completion of work on the operational base, the company's management team paid a courtesy call on Obi Nwako and informed him that the company would commence operation in their town in the following month. As a way of showing appreciation for the visit, the king and his wife hosted their visitors to a lavish reception. While the visitors were in the palace, the *igwe* made a lot of demands with the name of his town; without hesitation, the company's management promised to look into his demands and respond at the appropriate time. The company equally made some requests which the king promised to look into after due consultation with his people. The meeting ended on a happy note; and the visitors received royal souvenirs from the king, before they left the palace.

Obi Nwako and his wife escorted their visitors to their cars which were parked at the car park. The oil company's staff boarded their vehicles, and as they were driving out of Obi Nwako's compound, Youth leader and two youths came into the compound and hastened to meet Obi Nwako and his wife at the porch. Obi Nwako was surprised when he saw them coming toward him. Casting a glance at the big envelope in youth leader's hand, the king wondered why the three youths barged into his compound at that time. When the youths got closer to the royal couple, they paid obeisance to the king who instantly asked them to rise; without wasting time, the youths complied with the order.

"I hope all is well?" asked the king.

"*Igwe*, there is no problem," said the youth leader. "We brought application letters and curricula vitae of some of us that wish to work in Wise-East petroleum."

The king scratched his head and said: "That's all right ... that was part of the things I discussed with the company's management some minutes ago. Let me have what you brought."

Youth leader bowed and gave the envelope they came with to Obi Nwako and told him that it contained the application letters and curricula vitae of all the youth of Ogiga kingdom that wished to take up employment in Wise-East petroleum. As Obi Nwako received the envelope, he promised to do something about the youth's desire to work in Wise-East petroleum. Thereafter, he called one of his aides and gave him the envelope with ... the instruction that he should keep it on one of the stools in the royal chamber.

"Yes your highness," the aide said and collected the envelope from the king; bowed and hastened into the house with it.

"*Igwe,* we have to leave now," said the youth leader.

"So soon?" asked Obi Nwako. "Why the haste ...?"

"Your highness, we know you're a very busy man," said the youth leader. "We have to leave, so that you will have time to attend to other things."

"That's very thoughtful of you," said the king; and as he watched with his wife, the youths turned and happily left the compound. The royal couple walked back into their house after the youths had gone out of sight.

Okoro came to the palace in the evening of that same day that the youth leader et al, brought the youth's application letters and curricula vitae to Obi Nwako. The king was giving instruction to one of his aides when Okoro came in. On sighting Okoro, he discharged the aide. The aide bowed and left.

"*Igwe-ee!*" said Okoro.

"You're welcome, Chief Okoro."

"*Igwe*, you will reign forever."

"Thank you, Chief Okoro. Please sit down."

"Thank you, *igwe*," Okoro said and collapsed his weight into a seat. "How are the queen and the children doing?"

"They are fine," said Obi Nwako. "And ... how is your family?"

"We thank God," said Okoro. "Their problem is part of the reasons I came to see you."

"Problem?" asked Obi Nwako. "What could the problem be?"

Okoro told the king that his son came back the previous day, after completing the one year mandatory national youth service ... "He declared interest in working in the oil company we gave land to."

Obi Nwako giggled and asked: "Is that what you called problem?"

"I came with his curriculum vitae. We sincerely need your assistance, *igwe*."

"That's not a big deal. The oil company is on our land, hence they must give preference to indigenes of our town in the areas of employment and contracts etcetera. Let me have the curriculum vitae."

Okoro gave him the envelope he came with. Obi Nwako received the envelope from his visitor; and brought out the curriculum vitae that was in the envelope. After perusing the curriculum vitae, he said: "This is a good curriculum vitae and he graduated with good grade. I believe they must give him job."

"I will be very grateful, your highness, if they absorb him in their organisation," said an elated Okoro.

While the king was still discussing with Okoro, an aide came in and informed the *igwe* that the president general of Ogiga town union had come to see him.

"Let him in immediately," said the king.

"Yes your highness," the aide said, then he bowed and dashed out.

"Who knows what brought Aghanya to my palace today," Obi Nwako said to Okoro.

"Let's wait and see," responded Okoro.

Aghanya stepped in; while bowing to the king, he said: "May you live long your highness."

"Thank you, my president. I'm delighted to have you under my roof today. You are highly welcome ... Please sit."

"Thank you, your highness. Chief Okoro, I salute you."

"Thank you Aghanya," said Okoro.

"You're welcome," said Aghanya, who sat down almost immediately.

"My president, it is unusual for you to visit my palace," said Obi Nwako. "I hope all is well?" he asked.

"*Igwe*," said Aghanya, "all is well, but there seems to be confusion somewhere. I thank God that Chief Okoro is equally here."

Okoro and Obi Nwako looked at each other and shrugged. Aghanya cleared his throat and told them that he came because of the royalty Wise-East petroleum was supposed to pay to their town. More so, he told them that the initial bulk sum the company was supposed to pay them before erecting any structure on their land was not seen; and that tongues had started wagging. Obi Nwako became uncomfortable, but Aghanya went on to tell him that if nothing was done urgently, people would assume that they collected and used the money to better their individual lives.

"That's why I came to see you, your highness. Since you're the one that negotiated with them when they came, I want to know if you've been discussing issues relating to our money with them," Aghanya concluded.

Obi Nwako became confused; he scratched his head while staring at the wall that stood opposite him.

"*Igwe*, I think Aghanya has a point," said Okoro.

"Yes, yes, yes," said Obi Nwako. "He sure has a point. Don't worry yourself, Aghanya. I've discussed with them and they promised to pay."

"Your highness, when do they intend to send the cheque across," asked Aghanya.

The king slid into deep thought while tapping his fingers on his forehead. Okoro and Aghanya looked at each other in disbelief. Deep down in their minds, they sensed that something was wrong, thereafter, Aghanya begged to leave, but that was after he had begged Obi Nwako to table before Wise-East petroleum, all the complaints he had brought to the palace. Aghanya's takeaway from the meeting was a promise from the king that he would do as the president general had requested.

Seated on a settee in his sitting room, Obi Nwako intermittently sipped wine from a wine glass while watching television with his wife. With her head on his laps and a fashion magazine in her hand, his wife's attention was torn between the magazine in her hand and the programme being aired on television. As her attention oscillated from the fashion magazine which she perused intermittently to the television which engulfed her husband's attention, Williamson rushed in; he was panting and fuming. "Your highness, there is …" Instead of completing the sentence, he covered his eyes with his hands after seeing the king's wife lying on the settee with her head on her husband's laps. "Oh, I'm sorry. I'm sorry for invading your privacy," he said, while looking away.

Obi Nwako's wife sat up and greeted Williamson.

"Your highness, there's serious problem in town," said Williamson.

"Calm down first," said Obi Nwako.

In quick succession, Williamson breathed out heavily for two consecutive times … when he relaxed and began to breathe normal, Obi Nwako said: "Better."

The visitor hissed and shook his head.

"Why did you run into this place like someone being pursued by the harbinger of death?"

"Your highness, the youth … The youth are threatening to burn down my company's facility. They barricaded off the road that led to our base and manhandled some of my staff. They almost lynched me, your highness."

Obi Nwako and his wife were surprised … as they stared at each other, confusion began to brew in the king's head.

Oji ran into Isi-Ichie's compound in a manner reminiscence of a man whose house was on fire. His arrival coincided with Isi-Ichie's appearance at his house's main entrance.

"Isi-Ichie, Isi-Ichie," Oji shouted as he rushed closer to the nonagenarian. "There is problem," he said.

"Calm down Chief Oji … What troubles you?"

"*Nna anyi* [Elderly one], the youth of Ogiga kingdom are on rampage. They have set bonfire on the roads; and they are threatening to burn down the oil company's facility."

"Pull yourself together. Aghanya had already brought the report to me. I have sent him to fetch the youth for me."

Oji breathed out heavily … and turned when he heard the sound of a vehicle behind him. Obi Nwako's convoy of two vehicles came into the compound and parked. Oji and Isi-Ichie stared and thanked God [in their minds] for bringing the king to Isi-Ichie's compound at that moment.

The convoy was made up of a jeep and a Rolls Royce. While the two drivers remained in their vehicles, two armed policemen came down from the jeep and hastened to the Rolls Royce. The two policemen held open the back doors of the Rolls Royce for Obi Nwako and Williamson to alight from the car. Immediately they came down from the Rolls Royce, the king hastened to where Oji was standing with Isi-Ichie, while Williamson and the two policemen trailed behind him.

"Isi-Ichie, Isi-Ichie," Obi Nwako called with a low-pitched voice while moving closer to the old man that was highly revered by every indigene of Ogiga, irrespective of the indigene's status.

"*Nna anyi*, there is fire on the mountain," said Obi Nwako.

"Who set the mountain on fire?" asked Isi-Ichie.

Before Obi Nwako could answer the question, Williamson got closer and stood beside him, while the policemen kept their distance.

"Isi-Ichie, the youth are out there doing things that will retard the development of this kingdom if not checked. They've been hostile to strangers, and they are threatening to burn down things," said Obi Nwako.

Isi-Ichie et al. looked toward the gate and fixated their eyes on Aghanya's vehicle as it came into the compound ... and parked. Aghanya alighted from the vehicle and hastened to where Isi-Ichie and others were standing.

"Where are the youth?" asked Isi-Ichie. "I asked you to bring them along," Isi-Ichie said to Aghanya.

"*Nna anyi* [elderly one]," said Aghanya, "the scene out there is better imagined than experienced. The youth are deeply pained. They didn't want to listen to anyone. Every attempt made to pacify them was like pouring water on a rock."

Isi-Ichie slid into a deep thought, later he instructed Aghanya to go back to where the youth were protesting. Aghanya nodded in agreement; thereafter, Isi-Ichie emphatically said: "Tell them to come to this place immediately, or else … or else they will have themselves to blame."

"Yes *nna anyi*," said Aghanya with a bow. He turned and was hastily leaving to deliver the message to the protesting youth of Ogiga kingdom.

"One more thing," said Isi-Ichie.

Aghanya halted and turned back, "*Nna anyi*," he said.

"On your way back," said Isi-Ichie, "stop in at Chief Okoro's house and ask him to come with you immediately."

"Your wish is my command *nna-anyi*," Aghanya said and headed to his car.

When Aghanya entered his car and drove off, Isi-Ichie turned to Williamson and asked: "What is the cause of the problem between your company and the youth?"

"Honestly sir, I don't know. We don't have any problem with them. They've never brought any complain to us," said Williamson.

"How do you mean? Are you insinuating that our youth woke up and started destroying your things without provocation?" asked Isi-Ichie.

"That's how we saw it sir," said Williamson.

Isi-Ichie sternly told Williamson that Ogiga town was not known as a breeding place for unreasonable youth. "Nobody wakes up and rampage against an organisation without provocation."

Isi-Ichie turned to Obi Nwako, "*Igwe*," he called.

"*Nna anyi*, Isi-Ichie," answered Obi Nwako.

"Why are our children displaying their anger on the street?" asked Isi-Ichie.

"To be frank with you, *nna anyi*, I don't know. I went to talk to them but they didn't give me audience. In short, they would have stoned me, if not that I ran for my dear life," responded Obi Nwako.

"So it got to that extent?" asked Isi-Ichie.

"It's terrible, *nna anyi*," said Obi Nwako.

All eyes went to Isi-Ichie's lips after Obi Nwako's response. They expected the old man to say something, but he chose to brood and ... after awhile, he lifted his head and gazed at the sky.

Chants from the youth filtered into the compound, Isi-Ichie looked toward the gate and saw the youth rushing into his compound with green leaves in their hands; more so, firecrackers were blasting in their midst. Williamson panicked and ran round Isi-Ichie, while the youth ran round the compound. Aghanya's vehicle sped in ... and parked; while the youth were still running round the compound.

Okoro and Aghanya came down from the vehicle and hastily went and stood with Isi-Ichie and others. Still chanting, the youth went and stood before Isi-Ichie et al. Williamson became frightened the more because of the firecrackers that were still blasting from the youth's position.

"Do you really realise where you are?" Isi-Ichie asked the youth with a heart full of rage.

"Si-le-nce!" shouted the youth leader.

The youth kept quiet the moment their leader called for silence.

"No, go on, keep chanting," said Isi-Ichie; he turned almost immediately, and was about to leave in anger.

The youth knelt and apologised to Isi-Ichie, but the old man ignored their pleas and began to move …

"Chief Oji, please beg him for us," pleaded the youth leader.

Williamson was surprised by the turn of events; Oji had pity on the youth and accosted Isi-Ichie; and told him that his anger would complicate things. He further pleaded with the nonagenarian to forgive the youth even though they erred by not behaving themselves in his presence.

"They have accepted … and apologised for their folly. Nna anyi, the onus is now on you to forgive them, so that we will move forward," said Oji.

Isi-Ichie was touched by Oji's words; he looked at Oji, shook his head and went back with him. All the youth prostrated the moment Isi-Ichie got back to where he was standing before. Williamson was dumbfounded by what was happening. He never believed that anything could frighten the youth and make them to keep quiet. Isi-Ichie heaved a sigh and asked the youth to get up. The youth thanked him and happily stood up.

"What led to the recent madness?" he asked the youth leader.

Youth leader bowed and reassured Isi-Ichie of the youth's unflinching loyalty to him; he went further to apologise for their unruly behaviour. "We are very, very sorry, *nna anyi.*"

"That's all right. Answer my question," said Isi-Ichie.

"*Nna anyi,* the protest was caused by the nonchalant attitude of Wise-East petroleum toward the plight of the people of this kingdom," said the youth leader.

"What do you mean by that?" Oji asked the youth leader.

Youth leader told them that the youth embarked on the protest because oil spills caused by Wise-East petroleum's recklessness had destroyed aquatic lives and farmlands in their town. Hence, those of them that were fishermen could not fish again because the fishes were killed by oil which the oil company regularly spilled into their rivers. More so, the youth leader stated that those of them that were farmers could no longer go to farm again because their farmlands which were regularly submerged by oil were no longer arable. He went further to inform Isi-Ichie and the other persons present that Wise-East petroleum, never considered the indigenes of their town, whenever they were employing those that would work for them, and that the company had never done any project in their town as part of its corporate social responsibility.

When the youth leader was done speaking, Isi-Ichie asked Williamson to respond to all the allegations against his company. Williamson thanked Isi-Ichie for arresting the tension created by the misunderstanding between his company and the youth of Ogiga kingdom. The American acknowledged that oil spills occurred during their operations; he was also quick to add that it was never intentional; hence, their team of professionals often rushed to clean up oil spill whenever they got report of its occurrence.

Furthermore, Williamson claimed that they were recruiting both indigenes and non-indigenes since they commenced operation; and wondered why the youth would allege that they weren't giving jobs to Ogiga indigenes. "On corporate social responsibility," said Williamson, "I implore everyone to be patient with us. Very soon, you will see the wonders my company will do in that regard."

Isi-Ichie et al. almost sympathised with Williamson when he finished speaking, but the youth leader shattered that sympathy building up in them with a bombshell.

"My elders," said the youth leader, "they've been employing people since they commenced operation, but no indigene of this town is working in that company. All their staff … cleaners, gatemen, messengers, clerks, executive and management staff etcetera are strangers."

"Sorry, I have to come in here," said Williamson. "We don't directly employ people. We contracted it out to a consulting firm that hires and sends applicants to us after putting them through aptitude test and rigorous oral interview. We employ whoever they recommend to us irrespective of where the person comes from."

"Then what do we benefit from your company considering the environmental degradation you cause in our town?" asked Okoro.

"Obviously, there's need for a change of strategy so that we can address the youth's grievances," said Williamson.

"That will be appreciated if it will be possible," said Aghanya.

"We will make it possible, sir," said Williamson.

Isi-Ichie asked the youth leader if Williamson's proposition was okay by him and those he was leading. Youth leader responded with an emphatic, "No!" and went on to request that Williamson should tell them what his short, medium and long term plans for the town were. When Isi-Ichie asked Williamson to react to the youth leader's request, Williamson told them that for a start, his company would award scholarships to indigent students from Ogiga kingdom to go overseas and study courses relevant to his company's line of operation. He equally promised to arrange ad hoc employment exercise for natives of Ogiga only; also, he promised to give special consideration to natives of Ogiga in their next general recruitment exercise.

"And don't forget, in the long run, those we shall award scholarships to, will be the ones to pilot the affairs of Wise-East petroleum," said Williamson.

"Is that okay by the youth?" Isi-Ichie asked the youth leader.

"If they can keep their promise," said the youth leader, "then, they won't have problems with us again."

"One more thing," said Williamson, "as part of our social responsibility, we shall build administrative block and faculty building in the new state university which will be sited in this town."

"I think the problem has been solved," said Isi-Ichie.

Others concurred to what Isi-Ichie said.

"Can the enemies now become friends?" Isi-Ichie asked the youth leader.

Smiling, the youth leader bowed and said: "Yes, *nna anyi.*" Thereafter, he shook hands with Williamson and embraced him; while all the other youth shouted with joy.

CHAPTER TEN

Okoro visited Obi Nwako with his son, Onochie some weeks after Isi-Ichie brokered peace between Wise-East petroleum and Ogiga youth. The visit was prompted by Onochie's curriculum vitae which Okoro gave to the king, with the believe that the royal father would use his royal influence and connection to secure employment for the young man, in Wise-East petroleum; but to Okoro's family's consternation, no favourable news flew from the palace to them in that regard. Okoro told the king that peace had departed from his family because of his son's joblessness, and because the *igwe* had not given them any response, since he gave his son's curriculum vitae to him … for employment in Wise-East petroleum some months earlier.

"Your highness, Onochie has been so worried, and he has been wondering why securing employment for him in an oil company that is in our town could be so difficult for me, whereas people from other towns are given permanent employment by the same oil company," said Okoro.

The king listened with rapt attention to all that his friend had to say. Thereafter, he smiled and said: "Chief Okoro, you amuse me."

Obi Nwako's reaction did not go down well with Okoro. He was surprised; he wondered why his family's problem could be a source of amusement to the king.

"Have you not heard of global economic recession?" asked Obi Nwako.

"Your highness, I am aware of the global economic recession, but I can't see what it has got to do with my plea to you to secure job for my son in Wise-East petroleum."

"It has got a lot to do with it, Chief Okoro."

"How?" asked Okoro.

Obi Nwako told Okoro that the recession had led to reduction in the global work force; hence, Wise-East petroleum placed embargo on employment. He went on to inform his visitors that the oil company in their town was no longer recruiting; and that the order for them to suspend all forms of recruitment came from the oil company's parent company in the United States.

"Chief Okoro, you're my right hand man. Once Wise-East petroleum lifts embargo on employment, I will pressurise them to employ your son first."

"That's all right," said Okoro.

"Onochie," Obi Nwako called.

"Your highness," answered Onochie.

"Don't worry," said Obi Nwako, "they will employ you before anyone else."

"Thank you, your highness," said Onochie. "May God bless you," he prayed.

"And bless you too," responded Obi Nwako.

A royal aide came in and informed the king that Chief Kwocha and Chief Nnam had come from Agba kingdom to see him.

"Let them in," said Obi Nwako.

The aide bowed and left.

"Cheer up, Chief Okoro," said Obi Nwako.

"Well," said Okoro with a shrug, "let me hold you to your word."

The two chiefs from Agba kingdom stepped into the palace and saluted Obi Nwako with a bow. The king asked them to rise ... "You're welcome," he said to them as they complied with his directive.

"Thank you, your highness," said Kwocha.

As the visitors exchanged pleasantries with Okoro, he asked them a question that threw them off balance.

"How is that small boy that prides himself on being the *igwe* [king] of Agba kingdom?" asked Okoro. The two visitors were shocked by the question to the extent that they stared at each other with mouths agape. After awhile, they closed their mouths and shrugged.

"Chief Okoro, our *igwe* is not a small boy," said Nnam.

"Is that what you think?" asked Okoro, while grinning. "Well, those days at central school, I always beat him black and blue. I was his class monitor in primary five."

"Okay," said Kwocha.

"When you get home, tell him you saw Chief Okoro."

"We will gladly do that, sir," said Nnam.

"Chief Okoro, stop harassing my visitors," said Obi Nwako.

"I'm sorry your highness," said Okoro.

"Thank you," Obi Nwako said to Okoro. To his visitors, he said: "Please sit down."

"God bless you, your highness," said Kwocha, as he and Nnam sat on two different seats in the palace.

"I hope you came in peace?" asked Obi Nwako.

"Yes, your highness, we came in peace," said Kwocha. "We came to fulfil our promise to you."

"And what could the promise be?" asked Obi Nwako.

Nnam reminded Obi Nwako, that the day he came with Kwocha to plead with him to secure jobs for their children, in Wise-East petroleum that they promised to give him parcels, if he could make it possible for their sons to get jobs in the oil company that was based in Ogiga.

"Okay," said Obi Nwako.

"Your highness, we brought you that which we promised," said Nnam.

Obi Nwako gave signs to the visitors from Agba kingdom, but the two men did not get the message he was trying to pass across to them. Instead of holding on, they kept spilling the beans. Perhaps, the almighty God chose that day as the day he would expose Obi Nwako and let his people know that he had been selling their employment slot to strangers.

"Your highness, we promised that we will give you our children's furniture and wardrobe allowances if you could secure jobs for them in Wise-East petroleum," said Kwocha.

Obi Nwako became very uncomfortable ... because what his visitors from Agba kingdom wanted to do next would spoil a lot of things for him if Okoro should witness it; hence he kept giving the duo sign to hold on, but they ignored the signs.

"We came to fulfil our promise, your highness," said Kwocha.

While still standing, Kwocha winked at Nnam; the latter nodded and stood up. Both men brought out two fat envelopes from their pockets and moved closer to Obi Nwako. While Okoro and Onochie moped, the two chiefs from Agba kingdom presented the two envelopes which contained huge sums of money to Obi Nwako. Instead of being joyful, the king said in his mind that the ground ought to have opened and swallowed up the two men; and had the transaction botched.

"Your highness, here's the money," said Nnam.

Okoro and Onochie stood up and angrily left the palace, immediately Obi Nwako collected the envelopes from the two men. To Nnam and Kwocha's surprise, Obi Nwako muttered, "Hey," when Okoro left the palace with his son. The chiefs from Agba kingdom stood confused before the king ... they later asked Obi Nwako what the problem was, and why Okoro angrily left with his son. Instead of responding to his visitors' inquisition, Obi Nwako rested his forehead on his left palm and focused his gaze on the floor.

"I thought you said that the king is your friend," was the question Onochie asked his father after their disappointing visit to Obi Nwako. Okoro who was seated on one of the seats in his sitting room looked at his son with a face and eyes that were filled with regrets ... and thus he answered his son, "I thought he was my friend, but little did I know that I was riding on the back of a tiger. But all hope is not lost."

Onochie gave his father a pitiful look, shook his head and walked straight into his room.

Okoro could not eat well for days because he trusted Obi Nwako so much that he wouldn't have believed that the king would ever betray him. He wouldn't have believed it, if not that he witnessed the incident that unfolded in the palace … when the two chiefs from Agba kingdom brought money to Obi Nwako to show appreciation to him, for securing jobs for their sons in the oil company that was in their town; whereas, his son, Onochie's curriculum vitae was with the *igwe* [king], and he couldn't secure job for him in the same oil company that he had been helping strangers to get jobs in.

His predicament was worse than what his family imagined. In spite of all, he was burdened by his conscience. His greatest problem was how to report the atrocities of the *igwe* to his fellow chiefs, knowing fully well that he singlehandedly made Obi Nwako the *igwe* of Ogiga kingdom; despite opposition from many quarters. He felt that members of the council of kingmakers would laugh him to scorn if he should open his mouth and complain that he had fallen victim to Obi Nwako's treacherous acts, hence, he kept the king's evil acts to himself. He was dying In silence, but he comported himself and carried on as if all was well whenever he was with other chiefs.

"I am getting upset with Wise-East petroleum for deliberately denying us the royalties they are supposed to be paying to us, for their operations in our town," said Aghanya to the trio of Isi-Ichie, Okoro and Oji; as they sat in Isi-Ichie's compound examining some of the problems that bedeviled their town.

"I guess you've been meeting with them," said Isi-Ichie.

Youth leader stepped into the compound with two youths and headed straight to where the four men were seated. Aghanya told Isi-Ichie that he met with the officials of the oil company several times on the said matter; and that they kept telling him that they've been paying; and that the *igwe* would bear them witness.

"I've gone to the *igwe* several times to find out if they paid to him or to anyone he knows," stated Aghanya, "but on each occasion, the *igwe* dismissed me with incomprehensible tale. We have two other oil companies operating in our town. Those ones are not giving us problem. I wonder why this Wise-East petroleum chose to give us headache all the time."

Okoro was devastated by Aghanya's presentation. More so, all the shady deals of their king which he knew; and which he didn't want to say were greater burden to him. He hissed and shook his head in grief.

"I suspect conspiracy," said Oji.

"You're right, Chief Oji," said Okoro.

With a bow, the three youths greeted Isi-Ichie et al. when they got closer to them; they equally pledged their loyalty to the nonagenarian. Isi-Ichie welcomed them and asked them to sit down.

"Thank you, *nna-anyi*," said the youth leader.

As the youths sat down, Isi-Ichie gave sign to Oji who responded with a nod, and went on to clear his throat.

"Our people say that whenever the toad chooses to run in the afternoon that something is amiss," said Oji. "What brought the strength of our kingdom to this place; at this time?" Oji asked the youths.

Youth leader thanked them for accommodating him and the two youths he came with. Thereafter he thanked Oji for the question, and began thus: "Three years ago, when the youth protested against the exclusion policy of Wise-East petroleum..."

Aghanya cut in before the youth leader could complete the sentence. "What do you mean by that?" asked Aghanya.

The youth leader told them that he was talking about Wise-East petroleum's refusal to employ Ogiga indigenes in their establishment. While the chiefs nodded, the young man went on to inform them that during the youth protest three-years prior, the company promised to change their strategy so that they could employ natives of Ogiga ... and that the company reneged on that promise.

"They are still employing outsiders. Few of our people working in that company are casual workers. So the youth met and sent us to come and complain to Isi-Ichie," said the youth leader.

"You have done well," said Isi-Ichie.

"What the youth leader said is true," Okoro said, to the astonishment of all the people in Isi-Ichie's compound at that moment. But that was not all he wanted to tell them.

"Do you know that *igwe* Obi Nwako collects money from non-indigenes of this town and secure jobs for them in the oil company that is polluting our farmlands and rivers?" asked Okoro. "I am convinced that it is employment slots meant for our people that he sells to the outsiders," asserted Okoro.

The other people were shocked by the allegation levelled against Obi Nwako by his erstwhile friend; for this, they stared at him in disbelief.

"Why are you all looking at me as if you have seen a traitor?" asked Okoro.

"We were surprised to hear you sound the way you just did," responded Oji. "Obi Nwako's ascension to the throne was your project; and since his coronation, you have been his worthy ally," he concluded.

"But that does not mean I should keep quiet when he does something untoward," said Okoro. "After all I'm a chief; and an *ozo* title holder."

Isi-Ichie begged the youths to excuse them. Without wasting any time, the young men instantly complied with Isi-Ichie's directive. When the youths had gone out of hearing distance, Isi-Ichie told the chiefs that he had thought that the coming of the Wise-East petroleum would be a blessing to their town. He went on to regret that the company had chosen to often do things that tamper with the peace and unity of their town. He equally opined that the allegations against Obi Nwako by Aghanya and Okoro were grievous acts.

"Non-payment of royalties, and selling of our employment slots to people from other towns are serious allegations. We must have to do something urgently before the youth of this town go out of control," stated the Isi-Ichie.

Isi-Ichie's statement pleased his audience so much; ... Oji went on to suggest that they set up committee that would investigate Obi Nwako and Wise-East petroleum.

"I was in *igwe* Obi Nwako's palace," retorted Okoro, "when two chiefs from Agba kingdom brought money to him to thank him for securing jobs for their sons in Wise-East petroleum."

Okoro's claim was shocking. His audience would have doubted him if not that they knew how close he was to Obi Nwako. The meeting later requested Aghanya to try and get from

Wise-East Petroleum, details of all the payments they've made to their town since they started operation.

They scheduled to meet again in a fortnight with the hope that Aghanya would come with more details. They later called the youths back and begged them to bear with them for another one month. They claimed that they would need much time to look properly into the allegation the youths brought against Wise-East petroleum; and other allegations brought against the same company by some other persons. The youths thanked them and happily left while the men started discussing something else.

Okoro lay in his bed at night reflecting on events in their town since Obi Nwako became their *igwe*. He wondered why their *igwe* chose be so mischievous and unreliable. Nevertheless, he was still fair in his judgement to the point that he blamed himself for all that Obi Nwako had done since he became their *igwe*. The king's kinsmen and his mother's people failed to clear him for initiation into the *ozo* society, but he [Okoro] used his influence as the regent to lobby the kingmakers to amend the kingship constitution of Ogiga kingdom, to favour Obi Nwako. It was that constitutional amendment that made it possible for Obi Nwako to become *igwe* without being a member of the prestigious *ozo* society. Okoro's flow of thought was truncated by his phone's ring tone. He picked the phone and hissed when he noticed that Obi Nwako was the caller. After awhile, he hesitantly answered the call.

"Hello, your highness."

"I used to think that we were friends, but ..."

"What are you talking about, your highness?"

"No wise person backstabs his friend," said Obi Nwako. "I heard you vehemently spoke against me before Isi-Ichie and other chiefs. You even went as far as accusing me of selling employment slots meant for our people to indigenes of other towns."

"You glaringly did all that I accused you of," opined Okoro. "Please your highness, I am tired. I need some rest."

He ended the call; and ..., "Nonsense," he muttered and dropped his phone on a stool.

"Hello, hello," said Obi Nwako. "Chief, are you still there?" he asked, thinking that Okoro was still willing to talk with him. He dropped his phone when he realised that Okoro had long terminated the call.

The king breathed out noisily and said: "So it has gotten to this. Hmm; an enemy that was hitherto a friend, could be very dangerous." He stood up and shook his head; thereafter, he muttered, "Chief Okoro, I hope you can bear what you have brought upon yourself?"

Two days after Obi Nwako called and expressed his disappointment on Okoro, for telling some people that he was in the habit of selling to strangers, the employment slots meant for their people at Wise-East petroleum, Okoro and Aghanya went to the oil company to find out things for themselves. When the duo got to Williamson's office at Wise-East petroleum, they told him that their people sent them to find out from him his company's reason for refusing to pay royalty to Ogiga people; and why they weren't giving jobs to Ogiga indigenes despite his promise to them.

"Once again, you're welcome," said Williamson.

"Thank you," responded Aghanya.

"I appreciate your resolve to confront us peacefully on the issues you just raised," said Williamson.

As Okoro and Aghanya nodded, Williamson continued, "It baffles me that your people could peddle such malicious allegations against us, despite all we've been doing to better the lives of everyone in Ogiga town."

The two visitors were surprised by their host's claims; they looked at each other and shrugged. Then, Okoro snapped out of his confused state and said: "We would appreciate it if you could get specific."

"We have been paying royalty to your people," said Williamson. "And, we have been offering permanent employment to indigenes of your town. Your king can bear me witness."

"Whom have you been giving the royalty?" asked Aghanya.

"Excuse me," said Williamson ... he picked and flipped through a file. "I got it. We've been giving cheques for the royalty to Chiefs Okoro and Aghanya."

The emissaries from Ogiga kingdom were stunned; they astonishingly looked at each other with pouted mouths ... and wondered if they were dreaming or awake. Oblivious of the kind of commotion his last statement had caused in his visitors' heads, Williamson went on to tell them that the two men claimed to be executive members of Ogiga development union. Okoro snapped his fingers and asked Williamson if he could recognise the so called Chiefs Okoro and Aghanya if he saw them.

"Hold on," said Williamson; he picked the intercom and told the person on the other end to tell the head of finance to come to his office immediately. When he dropped the intercom he said to his visitors, "Sorry, the staff that had the responsibility of delivering the cheques to the two chiefs from your town is not on seat."

"Please don't be annoyed Mr. Williamson," said Aghanya.

"Oh … there's no cause for that," said Williamson. "Say whatever you want to say."

"Did you issue the cheques in favour of both men?" asked Aghanya.

"No," said Williamson, "the cheques were issued in favour of Ogiga development union."

"There's nothing like Ogiga development union," said Aghanya. "What we have is Ogiga town union."

"Really?" asked Williamson.

"Yes," responded Okoro.

"I am Aghanya, and he is Chief Okoro. We've never collected any cheque from your company."

"Don't worry yourselves," said Williamson. "We shall liaise with the bank to find out the identities of the signatories to the account in which the cheques were paid into. I hope that will be fine by you."

Okoro and Aghanya responded in the affirmative, thereafter, they thanked their host and rose from their seats … Williamson saw them off to the passage and promised to keep them posted if his company stumbled on any information that might be useful to them in their investigation.

The two men appreciated their host's show of concern before leaving the office complex of Wise-East petroleum. Immediately the duo left, Williamson went back to his office and continued with what he was doing prior to their arrival. After some time, he stopped what he was doing and stared into space wondering the kind of problem Ogiga people were having that made them to send emissaries to come and find out some things from him.

CHAPTER ELEVEN

"*Iwe-Iwe-Iwe* ... *Iwe!*" they chanted as they marched on the only road that led in and out of Ogiga town. "*Iwe*" means anger ... Ogiga youth were visibly angry as they protested against the shady activities of Wise-East petroleum in their town. The youth were led in that protest by their leader. Some of them were with placards while others armed themselves with green leaves. Okoro's car ran into them at a junction; they blocked the way and kept chanting, "*Iwe-Iwe-Iwe* ... *Iwe!*" The car pulled up ... and what separated the car from the protesting young men was a space measuring about fifteen feet. Thinking that what was happening before him was a tea party, Okoro alighted from his car to address the angry youth.

"Youth of Ogiga kingdom, I salute you."

The youth stopped chanting, but they did not respond to the greeting that came from Okoro.

"What troubles you this day?" asked Okoro.

"We are protesting against the Wise-East petroleum's refusal to give jobs to our people; and against their refusal to pay royalty to our town," said the youth leader.

A youth told Okoro that they heard that the chiefs sold to strangers, employment slots meant for Ogiga indigenes in Wise-East petroleum. Okoro suggested that the youth should see the *igwe* [king] and ask him about their employment slots in Wise-East petroleum. "The *igwe* is the only person the oil company collects names from," he said.

"But *igwe* Obi Nwako has been your ally," said another youth. "And you single-handedly made him the *igwe* despite protests by the people."

While Okoro stuttered in his bid to answer the question, two youths went and stood behind him.

"*Ehm, ehm,* you know … one man cannot install an *igwe,*" said Okoro.

"Liar!" shouted one of the youths standing behind Okoro.

The chief was shocked, he wanted to turn and see the person that called him a liar; but before he could do that, he got a kick from the rear. He fell to the ground. As he groaned in pain, they lifted him above their heads. While they marched on, they sang, "*Tufuo nu nwa melu aru; orue echi amuta ozo* [Throw away the evil child; another child will be given birth to, tomorrow]" Intermittently, they pinched him as they moved forward; and on his part, Okoro screamed whenever he received a pinch from any of them.

Okoro experienced in the hands of the young men, what he never imagined would ever come his way. The youth held him hostage until late in the evening, when they were done with their protest.

An emergency meeting of all the red cap chiefs in Ogiga was convened in Isi-Ichie's compound, shortly after Okoro's release by the youth. Obi Nwako was also in the meeting, likewise the members of his cabinet. One striking thing about Obi Nwako's kingship was the fact that he relegated the members of his cabinet to the background. He gave no function to any of them. He discharged his responsibilities as a king alone without seeking advice or input from his cabinet. His cabinet was more of ceremonial than functional. The king sidelined them in everything because of the nefarious activities he was involved in, and because of his inordinate love for money. Moreover, greed made him swear never to share the largesse from Wise-East petroleum with anyone.

In the meeting, that was held in Isi-Ichie's compound, the youth were represented by their leader and two other youths. Okoro was also in the meeting with bandages tied on his head and on his arm. Every other person in the meeting was seated except the three youths. They looked sober while standing before the chiefs and elders. Isi-Ichie furiously took a swipe on the trio for daring to rough handle Okoro. "What you people did is sacrilegious. Do you want to bring curse upon yourselves and upon the land?"

The three youths looked remorseful while Isi-Ichie stared at them.

"*Nna-anyi* [Elderly one], we are really sorry," said the youth leader. "We don't know what came over us."

Pointing at Okoro, the nonagenarian said: "Look at what you did to him. You beat up a chief; an elderly person and you stand here telling us you didn't know what came over you. This kind of act cannot possibly be swept under the carpet. You people must be sanctioned."

Fear gripped the youths when Isi-Ichie stated that they would be sanctioned. Isi-Ichie breathed out heavily and said: "You deserve to be banished."

The three youths fell on their knees instantly and began to plead for forgiveness. "*Nna-anyi*, please forgive us," the youth leader pleaded.

Williamson drove into the compound and parked his vehicle while Isi-Ichie was still contemplating on what to do with the youth of Ogiga town. Williamson came down from his vehicle with a file and moved toward the chiefs and elders that were there seated.

"Get out," said Isi-Ichie to the youths. "We shall later tell you what your punishment will be."

The three youths got up and as they dejectedly headed toward the gate, Williamson got closer and greeted Isi-Ichie, the elders and the chiefs with a bow. Isi-Ichie gave sign to Oji.

"You are welcome, Mr. Williamson," said Oji. "Please sit down."

Williamson thanked Oji for his kind gesture but he rejected the seat, and told him that he had little time to spend with them.

"I came because of the barrage of allegations that has trailed my company's operation in your community."

From the file he was holding, the American brought out a paper on which was printed two passport sized images of two different men.

"These two men have been ... on behalf of your town union collecting from us, cheques for the royalty we're supposed to pay to your town."

He gave the paper to Isi-Ichie who shook his head after looking at the photographs.

"I don't know any of these men," said Isi-Ichie before passing the paper on to Oji for his perusal. When Oji failed to recognise any of the two faces that appeared in the photograph, he shrugged and passed the paper to another person. The paper was passed onto many chiefs and elders, but none of them knew any of the two faces; until the paper got into Okoro's hand.

Okoro looked at the photographs and chuckled, "These are *Igwe* Obi Nwako's aides."

Others were surprised, but Obi Nwako rose angrily and flared-up.

"So Chief Okoro, it has gotten to the stage that you can smear my image, even in my presence?"

"*Igwe,* we know each other very well," said Okoro. "I have seen you with these men several times. They are regular visitors to your palace."

"This kingdom has no other king except my humble self. People frequent my palace for one reason or the other. That someone visited my palace does not mean that the person is my cohort. Please Chief Okoro, bridle your tongue. I beg of you."

Williamson brought out another paper from his file.

"This is the list of your sons and daughters we've given permanent employment."

"Let me have the list," said Aghanya, who instantly collected the list from Williamson ... he went on to peruse the list. "Those that bear these names are not from this kingdom," he said and passed the list onto another person. All that went through the list complained that none of the owners of those names was from Ogiga.

"We don't know any of them," said Williamson. "We do collect names from the king."

When the list got to Oji, he shook his head after perusing it ... he later muttered something to Isi-Ichie before speaking thus: "Truly, *Igwe,* the names here are not from this kingdom."

"I don't know," said Obi Nwako. "I sent names of our people to the company's human resources manager. I think he should be in a better position to tell us why our people are not given jobs in the company."

"*Igwe,* stop beating about the bush," said Okoro. "Tell them you sold our town's employment quota to outsiders."

"Chief Okoro, this your accusation is getting too much," said Obi Nwako. "Restrain your tongue; or..."

"Or you do what?" inquired Okoro.

Williamson became uncomfortable, "I have to go now," he said; and bowed to Isi-Ichie before moving toward his jeep ...

"Take care ... Mr. Williamson," said Oji.

"Thank you," replied Williamson.

Obi Nwako became livid with rage. His eyes oscillated between Okoro's face and Isi-Ichie's face; while the other chiefs focused their gaze on Williamson who was entering his jeep. When Williamson drove out of the compound, the chiefs and the elders looked at each other in disbelief and snapped their fingers.

In less than a week, after Williamson exposed Obi Nwako's sharp practices in a meeting with Isi-Ichie and other elders and chiefs, two staff of Wise-East petroleum ran into kidnappers. Tucker was behind the wheel while Serena was seated in the passenger's seat in front; as they cruised in a jeep on which their company's corporate identity was embossed. From afar, they sighted what looked like an accident scene; they saw a man and a motor bike lying on the road. The man was lying face down with crash helmet on his head. There was bloodlike substance on the ground ... very close to his head.

The company's vehicle pulled up few metres before the man and his revving motor bike. Tucker alighted from the jeep with Serena. As both of them rushed to help the presumed accident victim, two masked armed men came out from the bush. The two Americans were rushing to help the man on the ground without knowing that the masked men were coming to them from the rear.

The Americans got closer to the man that lay on the ground.

"Hello! Are you okay?" asked Tucker.

The man did not respond to Tucker's inquisition and ... neither did he move his body.

"This is serious," Tucker said to Serena. "Give me a hand; let's take him to the hospital."

To their astonishment, the man they came to help turned and pointed a gun at them. Tucker and Serena were frightened. They froze and quaked .... The man's face was covered with a mask.

"We're only trying to help," said Tucker; who was already fidgeting. "We thought you're an accident victim."

They turned to run, but got frozen when they saw the two armed masked men coming toward them. Their hearts pounded faster than normal ... and their blood pressure shot up immediately. The man they came to help got up from the ground, removed and dropped his helmet on the ground; but he did not remove his mask.

From behind, the man that was hitherto on the ground tied Tucker and Serena's eyes with black cloths. Thereafter, they marched the duo to the company's vehicle which they drove to the scene. Serena was made to sit on the passenger's seat in front, while Tucker was sandwiched between the two other masked men on the back seat. The masked man that was used as bait to get Serena and Tucker sat behind the wheel. He turned on the ignition ... and the vehicle screeched off.

Williamson barged into the palace panting while Obi Nwako was having meeting with his cabinet.

"Your highness, my company is in the middle of the storm once again."

"And, what is the problem this time around?" asked Obi Nwako.

"Your highness, two of my staff, Mr. Tucker and Miss Serena are missing."

"Where did it happen? ... and when did it happen?" asked Obi Nwako in astonishment.

"It happened in this town, your highness. It happened yesterday; in the evening hours. Their abductors are demanding one million United States dollars, or they kill the two of them."

Obi Nwako was shocked. "What?" he asked; and rose in anger. "How could that happen in this great kingdom?"

"Your highness," said Williamson, "it happened in this kingdom."

"Hey!" shouted Obi Nwako, who later slid into a deep thought. After awhile, he snapped his fingers and folded his hands. "What is my kingdom turning into?" he asked rhetorically. Turning to Williamson, he asked, "Have you informed the police?"

"No, your highness," answered Williamson.

"Why?"

"The kidnappers warned us not to involve any of the security agencies, unless we don't want to see Tucker and Serena alive again. They said they will be monitoring every move of ours; but we have informed the United States embassy."

"Good," said Obi Nwako with a worried face.

The king sat back on the throne and ruminated over the complaint brought to him by Williamson. After some time, he scratched his head with his hand and heaved a sigh. "What do we do now?" he asked, but to no one in particular.

His cabinet members wanted to make suggestions but he asked them to keep their cool that he knew what to do. He brought out his phone and made some calls; thereafter, he got up from the throne. "Come with me," he said to Williamson.

Members of his cabinet stared with mouths agape while he left the palace with Williamson.

Isi-Ichie woke up late that particular day. He had fever the previous day and was advised to have a good rest after taking his medication. Because of that, he didn't bother to rise from the bed early; and no member of his household bothered him. He was seated in his compound at mid-morning, with kola nut in his hand praying for peace and progress in Ogiga kingdom, when Oji rushed into the compound panting and fuming. Obi Nwako's jeep drove into the compound almost immediately. Obi Nwako was behind the wheel while Williamson was seated on the passenger's seat in front. The duo alighted from the vehicle after it pulled up beside one of the trees in Isi-Ichie's compound.

Oji got closer to Isi-Ichie ... he stood and watched Isi-Ichie who was still praying with kola in his hand. Obi Nwako and Williamson went and stood beside Oji ... Isi-Ichie concluded his prayer and broke the kola nut. He put the pieces in a small plate that was placed on a table that was set before him. Later, he cleared his throat and picked a piece of kola nut from the small plate.

"*Nna anyi, Isi-Ichie, ekene m gi* [Our father..., I salute you]," said Oji with a bow.

"Isi-Ichie, *ekene m gi* [... I salute you]," said Obi Nwako, who equally bowed to show reverence to the nonagenarian.

"You are all welcome," said Isi-Ichie. "You meet me well. Please sit down and take kola nut.

"I don't think I need to chew kola nut now," was Oji's response. "*Nna anyi,* there is problem."

"What happened?" asked Isi-Ichie. "My ears are itching."

"I was robbed about an hour ago, by three armed masked men," said Oji.

Isi-Ichie was shocked by Oji's claim, so also were Obi Nwako and Williamson. The trio stared sympathetically at the robbery victim for some time, then, Isi-Ichie decided to ask him some questions. "Where did it happen?"

"Not too far from my house," answered Oji. "They made away with my car, some cash, mobile phone, document and other valuables."

"Have you informed the police?" asked Isi-Ichie.

"Yes, *nna anyi*. They promised to bring the culprits to book."

"That means ... we now live with armed robbers in this town," said Isi-Ichie.

"*Nna anyi*," said Obi Nwako, "we're equally here with similar complain."

Isi-Ichie and Oji looked at Obi Nwako in surprise. The king breathed out heavily and continued. "Two staff of Wise-East petroleum were abducted in this town yesterday ... their kidnappers are demanding one million United States dollars as ransom."

Oji and Isi-Ichie were dumbfounded; thereafter, the latter pulled himself together ... after a while he asked Williamson if he had reported the incident to the police.

"We haven't informed the police, sir," was Williamson's response.

"Why?" asked Isi-Ichie.

"The kidnappers asked us not to do so, if we still wish to see the abductees alive," answered Williamson.

"Hey! *Alu!*[Sacrilege]" exclaimed Isi-Ichie.

After a cursory thought over the complaint brought before him, the nonagenarian asked the king to work with Williamson and make sure that the two abducted staff of Wise-East petroleum were released by their abductors. "More so, the kingdom will be expecting you to come up with permanent solution to this menace," added Isi-Ichie.

"Count on me *nna anyi*. I will not disappoint the kingdom," Obi Nwako promised. "I think I have to swing into action immediately," he further said.

"Better," said Isi-Ichie.

Obi Nwako picked kola nut from the plate that was on the table that was before Isi-Ichie and said to Williamson, "Come with me."

Williamson followed the king to his jeep; as they were driving out from the compound, Oji picked kola nut from the same plate and threw it into his mouth.

Aghanya's wife was in the kitchen preparing meal for her household; while her husband was in the bedroom resting. Suddenly, there was a bang on the entrance door to their house. She quickly washed her hands, picked the hand towel and stepped out of the kitchen, while still drying her hands with the hand towel. The bang on the door continued, she moved back and hung the hand towel on the kitchen door. The bang intensified. "I am coming," she shouted and headed to the door.

Aghanya appeared on the landing that was on the flight of steps that was in the house. From there, he watched as his wife went to open the door.

"Who is there?" asked Mrs. Aghanya. She strained her ears and asked again, "Who-o?"

She unlocked the door; before she could open it, the door was forcefully pushed open from outside. She staggered to one side. Her husband wanted to shout at those that pushed the door open, but he gave himself wise counsel when he saw that the three visitors were armed and at the same time masked. The masked men stepped into the sitting room; Aghanya pulled back and stealthily went into hiding while his wife fidgeted before the masked men. At gun point, they asked the woman of her husband's whereabouts. She told them that her husband was in his room upstairs.

"How many of you are in this house right now?" asked one of the masked men.

"My husband and I are the only ones at home."

"Sure?" asked the masked man.

"Yes sir," she answered.

They pushed and asked her to take them to where her husband was; that was after they had locked the entrance door. She led the way and they followed her up the stairs; when they got to the front of Aghanya's room, she stopped and pointed at the door, "He is in there." Two of the masked men forced the door open; they all stepped into the room and saw nobody in there. They looked weirdly at Mrs. Aghanya.

"I swear," she said, he was in here when I went to the kitchen downstairs."

They checked the wardrobe, the toilet and bathroom; yet, they saw no one in any of those places.

The two masked men that forced the door open were later asked by their leader to search all the other rooms in the building. The duo agreed and moved to search the other rooms while their leader remained in Aghanya's room with Mrs. Aghanya. Search conducted in the other rooms, wardrobes, toilets and bathrooms yielded no positive result. The duo that conducted the search went back to their leader, and informed him that there was no other person in the building.

The leader of the masked men turned to Aghanya's wife and asked: "Do you think we came here to play games with you?"

"I swear, my husband was in this house when you came in."

"Shut up!" screamed the leader...

"Yes sir," she responded, while shivering.

"Bring him out for us…," the leader said, and began to advance toward her.

Still shivering, she said: "I don't know where he's gone to. I swear."

Aghanya was listening to the conversation from where he was hiding in the ceiling. The leader of the masked men admired his wife while she shivered.

"You're a pretty woman," he said to her. "Your husband has an eye for good thing."

He grabbed her and put his lips to hers. She pushed him away; slapped and spat at him. The other two masked men wanted to descend on her, but their leader asked them to freeze. The duo halted.

"Don't touch her," said their leader … who began to remove his dress. Having only his boxers short on, he moved closer to Mrs. Aghanya.

"Please don't do this to me. I'm menstruating," she said while moving back.

"Lovely," said the man. "I love doing it with menstruating women."

In the ceiling where he was taking refuge, Aghanya became furious and wanted to rush down … but he halted after a rethink. He slid into a deep thought and remembered the encounter he had with his son, Afam, the day the boy came back with fireworks.

It happened that on that fateful day, Afam came back with a shopping bag and greeted his father who was watching television in the sitting room. A furious looking Aghanya sat up and asked him where he was coming from.

"I'm coming from the super market," answered Afam, who was in class three in the junior secondary [high] school.

"What did you go to the super market to do?"

"...to buy fireworks for Christmas."

"You went and bought fireworks?" asked Aghanya.

Afam nodded and said: "Yes dad."

"Your end of term examinations will begin next week; and you still have time to go and buy fireworks. Now, go and keep those things."

"Yes dad," said Afam ... thereafter, the boy headed toward the staircase.

"Be ready to provide them whenever I ask you to do so," said Aghanya.

Afam halted and said: "Yes dad."

"Did I make myself clear?" asked Aghanya.

"Yes dad."

"And where do you intend to keep those things?"

"I want to keep them in my room."

"You may go."

"Thank you, sir," Afam said, and climbed the flight of steps that was in the house.

"Nonsense," said Aghanya with a hiss.

In the ceiling where he was hiding, Aghanya nodded and said to himself, "I know what to do," then he moved toward the opening in the ceiling. Through the opening, he climbed down from the ceiling and found himself in the passage. From there, he moved to Afam's room.

Aghanya panicked as he searched Afam's room for the fireworks he asked the boy to keep. He searched the drawers, the wardrobe and even the toilet; but he did not see the fireworks. Apparently frustrated by the futility of the search he made, he scratched his head ... as confusion took hold of him. He wanted to exit the room, but on a second thought, he halted ... and lifted the mattress that was on Afam's bed. Lo and behold, the bag in which his son put the fireworks was under the mattress. He breathed in and out loudly before opening the bag. "Thank you Lord," he said when he saw packets of fireworks in the bag. He later picked the bag and moved out of the room.

In Aghanya's room, the leader of the masked men tore Mrs. Aghanya's dress and pushed her to the bed. The woman closed her eyes tight as the masked man made to pull down his boxers short; but before he could do that, gunshot like sounds rented the air. Shocked by the sound they were hearing, the masked men forgot about the woman and looked at each other in surprise. They picked their guns and positioned themselves for assault. Mrs. Aghanya coiled herself on the bed shivering, while the gunshot like sound continued unabatedly. The three masked men quietly left the room.

The three masked men came out from Aghanya's building, threw away their guns and ran toward their car that was parked at a corner in the compound. Their leader was still in his boxers short. He left his trousers and his shirt in Aghanya's room while running out to save his life. The trio opened their car's doors, but before they could enter the car, they heard a louder sound. The sound was like that of an artillery gun; it intensified the fear in them; because of that, they abandoned their car in Aghanya's compound and sprinted away.

"Nincompoops," said Aghanya, who watched from a window as the masked men ran out of his compound without their car. He remembered his wife and shouted ... He closed the window blind and ran out of the room.

When Aghanya rushed into his room, he saw his wife shivering with her head buried in her hands as she lay on the bed. She shrieked and shrank when Aghanya touched her. He turned her and discovered that her eyes were tightly closed.

"Please don't do this to me. Please ..." she said.

"It's me, honey."

Her body shook when she heard her husband's voice; afterwards she quietly opened her eyes.

"It's you," she said.

"Yes, it's me."

Sobbing, she sat up and put her head on her husband's shoulder. Aghanya held her.

"It is okay," he said to her.

She nodded and held him tight.

The three masked men ran into their den breathing heavily and noisily.

"It was like the man invited a battalion of the army," said the leader of the masked men.

"Thank God, we escaped alive," said another masked man while removing his mask.

The three masked men thanked God that they escaped from Aghanya's house alive, without knowing that the sounds they heard weren't from lethal weapons, but from fireworks.

Attempts to track the three masked men down with the vehicle they abandoned in Aghanya's compound proved abortive; because the police discovered during investigation, that the vehicle was stolen from a law abiding citizen [by the three masked men].

CHAPTER TWELVE

"We have been able to secure the release of the two kidnapped staff of the oil company ... after paying the sum of one million United States dollars to their abductors," said Obi Nwako, as he addressed prominent indigenes of Ogiga kingdom in Isi-Ichie's compound. Those that attended the meeting paid serious attention to what the king was saying. The attendees included Isi-Ichie, Okoro, Aghanya, Oji, Ndi-Ichie, Ozo title holders and other members of the council of kingmakers of Ogiga kingdom etcetera. As they listened, Obi Nwako condemned the raid on Aghanya's house by unknown armed men. "We equally thank God for giving him the wisdom to do what he did with the fireworks bought by his son. If not, the story would have been much more distasteful and horrible."

The king's audience adjusted their sitting positions when he told them that the *Igwe*-in-council had come up with a strategy to curtail crime and brigandage in Ogiga. "We want to set up a vigilante group in this kingdom, to put an end to atrocious crimes that are being committed in our town on a daily basis. We came up with the idea of setting up a vigilante group because we believe and know that the criminals terrorising us are human beings and they live amongst us."

His audience nodded and joyfully whispered to one another.

When Obi Nwako finished his address, Isi-Ichie asked the other people to react to all that the king had said; but no one spoke a word until he made the request for the second time. He equally expressed surprise that they weren't paying attention to what the king was saying. Thereafter, some persons decided to make contributions ... all of them spoke in favour of the king's proposal. The meeting later voted unanimously for the establishment of a vigilante group that would combat criminality in their town.

The two policemen that were attached to Obi Nwako watched with awe as members of Ogiga kingdom vigilante shoot at each other, while dancing in a circular form in Obi Nwako's compound. What surprised the policemen most was the fact that the vigilante men were not putting on any formal bullet proof vest; yet the bullets weren't penetrating their bodies. Tied to the waists of the vigilante men were scabbards that contained machetes. Two new buses with the inscription, "Ogiga Kingdom Vigilante" ... were parked in the compound. As the vigilante men danced and displayed their strength, Obi Nwako came out from the palace with Okoro, Aghanya and Oji.

Scorpion who was the head of the vigilante group gave sign to his boys immediately the king et al. came out from the palace. In obedience to Scorpion's directive, the vigilante men stopped dancing; and instantly fired some shots in the air.

"I can see that you guys are equal to the task," said Obi Nwako.

The king looked at the chiefs that were with him; they nodded, then the king continued, "With the powers conferred on me as the king of this kingdom, I hereby commission and give you power to sniff out every criminal in this kingdom without fear or favour. If you encounter any difficulty in any way, contact me or any of these chiefs."

While the vigilante men nodded to show agreement to all that the king had said, Obi Nwako called Scorpion.

"Yes, your highness," answered Scorpion, as he bowed.

"Lead them out for operation. Show no mercy to any criminal you find on our land," said Obi Nwako. "Make sure you comb every nook and cranny of this kingdom."

"Your wish is our command, your highness," said Scorpion. "We will not let you down; neither shall we disappoint the kingdom."

"Good," said Obi Nwako.

"Boys!" shouted Scorpion. "Move it!"

All the vigilante men rushed into the two buses that were parked in the compound, Scorpion entered one of the buses and sat on the passenger's seat in front. Obi Nwako's gateman hastily opened the gate ... the vigilante men shot in the air as the buses sped out of the compound. The chiefs standing with the king quivered while the shots were being fired; but an elated Obi Nwako asked them to relax that the vigilante men meant no harm.

About seventy-two hours after the inauguration of Ogiga kingdom vigilante group, the vigilante men paraded a rapist, two burglars, five vandals; and a hemp seller who was also a gun-runner before the chiefs and elders of Ogiga kingdom. The venue was Isi-Ichie's compound and a lot of people came to catch glimpse of those that swore never to let them have peace in their community. Scorpion ordered all the suspects to sit on the ground; they all complied except the hemp seller. Scorpion tried to force the hemp seller to sit on the ground, but instead of obeying him, the hemp seller attacked Scorpion and attempted to escape.

The hemp seller would have succeeded in running out of the compound, but for the vigilante man that shot him in the leg. When the bullet hit his leg, the hemp seller fell down and groaned in pain; but that did not deter the vigilante men from dragging him to the centre of the compound. They left him there ... his profuse bleeding notwithstanding. The elders and the chiefs were stunned; some of them later praised the vigilante men for their doggedness.

Members of the king's cabinet gathered In the palace for a meeting with the king of Ogiga kingdom. Some minutes into the meeting, an aide came in and informed Obi Nwako that emissaries from Ngodo kingdom had come to see him. The king appeared surprised, but after a little thought over what the aide said, he ordered that the emissaries be allowed to come in and see him.

"Yes, your highness," the aide said ... bowed and rushed out of the king's presence.

After some time, the emissaries from Ngodo came in and saluted the king with a bow. They equally paid compliments to the cabinet members before introducing themselves. The emissaries were four in number and their names were Uduezue, Chima, Chinweoke and Ikedi.

"To what do I owe this visit?" asked Obi Nwako.

"We are representatives of the four clans that make up Ngodo town," said Uduezue. "Our people sent us to you."

"What for?" asked Obi Nwako.

Uduezue told Obi Nwako that Ngodo people discovered that Wise-East petroleum was building its senior staff quarters on a land that belonged to Ngodo town, and that the company's management claimed that the land was given to them by

Ogiga kingdom. He went further to inform Obi Nwako that the oil company said that they had paid compensation for the said land [to Ogiga kingdom].

"Our people chided them for making spurious claims, but they swiftly debunked our assertion and advised us to seek clarification from you, your highness," stated Uduezue.

Obi Nwako smiled and took a swipe on the emissaries. He told them that he thought they came for something meaningful and serious. His ranting surprised the emissaries and the cabinet chiefs, but he didn't give a damn. He went on to tell the emissaries that he was in the know that his people gave the land in question to Wise-East petroleum for the construction of the company's senior staff quarters. The emissaries were shocked; they touched each other, probably to confirm that they weren't dreaming.

"Nevertheless, you came at the right time," said Obi Nwako. "My cabinet and I have been thinking of how to contact you people. The oil company just paid compensation for the said land; we were discussing sharing formula before you people arrived."

The cabinet members were dazed because they knew nothing about the land in question, and they weren't discussing compensation or sharing formula; but they dared not speak for fear of attracting the king's ire.

"*Igwe*, we are lost," said Uduezue.

Obi Nwako went on to tell them that the compensation paid by the oil company would be divided into two parts. He stated that forty percent of the money would go to Ngodo town, while the remaining sixty percent would be his, because he was the one that provided security for the oil company's staff and property. His cabinet members were irked ... they would have called him to order if not that he was harsh on some of them that tried to correct him in the past. The men from

Ngodo were stunned by the sharing formula proposed by Obi Nwako. They put their heads together and asked Uduezue to communicate their decision to their host.

Uduezue cleared his throat and said to Obi Nwako, "Your highness, we have heard what you said. If we were to decide, we would have said no to your proposal ..."

Obi Nwako was shocked, he began to fume; but Uduezue continued, "We will take your proposal to our people; we shall get back to you when they take decision on it."

"Go! Just go," said Obi Nwako, with an angry voice.

The emissaries bowed and left the king's presence while the king panted. Obi Nwako discharged members of his cabinet some minutes after the emissaries from Ngodo town left his palace; thereafter, he sent for Scorpion before moving into his room.

When Scorpion came to the palace he waited for many minutes before the king came out to see him. On sighting the king, he rose from his seat and greeted him.

"May you live long, your highness," he said, and bowed to show reverence to the king.

"I sent for you," said the king. "I have some problems ... and I want you to help me out."

"I am always at your service, your highness. What could the problems be?"

"Some people feel that the crown is too big for my head, and they've vowed to take it off my head."

"Who could the clowns be? Give me names *igwe*, and let's give them the treatment they deserve."

Like a thief, the king looked round to make sure no one was within hearing distance; then he brought out a paper from his pocket. Giving the paper to Scorpion, he said: "These are names and addresses of my adversaries."

Scorpion collected and perused the paper.

"Start sleeping well *igwe*, we shall teach these ones some lessons in the language they will understand."

Obi Nwako gave two hundred thousand naira to Scorpion and asked him to share same with his boys. After receiving the money, Scorpion thanked the king immensely; he equally prayed that Obi Nwako should reign forever.

"Remember," said the king, "you must do a clean job."

"Count on me your highness," said Scorpion ... he turned and left with the paper and the money.

Obi Nwako smiled and proudly said to himself, "Nothing compares to power. Whoever opposes my wish is going against a moving train."

Scorpion and some of his men barged into Uduezue's house; while Uduezue and his wife were savouring a delicious meal prepared by the woman.

"Are you Uduezue?" asked Scorpion; with a rude voice.

"Who are you? ... What gave you the audacity to barge into my house the way you just did?"

"Get up and follow us now!" ordered Scorpion.

"Is something wrong with you?" asked Uduezue. "By the way, who are you?"

"Well, if it will interest you ... we are vigilante men," said Scorpion. "We are here to arrest you for gun-running. We arrested some criminals who claimed that they rented guns from you. They've made useful confessions which implicated you."

Uduezue rose angrily with unwashed hands, pointing a finger at Scorpion he said: "You must be out of your mind. Get out of my house now!"

Scorpion sought to know what would happen if he refused to leave the place as commanded by Uduezue, but the man didn't have answer for such question. He then asked his men to arrest Uduezue. Unknown to Scorpion and his men, Uduezue was a brave man; he slapped the first vigilante man that touched him. All the vigilante men descended on him while Scorpion watched. Mrs. Uduezue rushed to rescue her husband, but the vigilante men pushed her away and beat her husband to a pulp before tying his hands together behind him. As they dragged Uduezue out of the house, his wife rushed after them screaming. Scorpion gave the woman a harsh slap and ordered her to go back. The woman became lethargic... As they put her husband in their vehicle and drove off, she staggered and fell.

Mrs. Ikedi's bar was a convergence point for fun seekers in Ngodo town. As usual people gathered there in the evening to eat, have some drinks and enjoy good music being played by the live band that often entertained customers that flocked the bar for merrymaking. Some of the customers were seated outside while others were in the bar. Those that had been served were either eating or drinking; while those not yet served waited patiently for Mrs. Ikedi and her staff to serve them.

Mrs. Ikedi came outside with food and drink placed on a tray. She was going to the customer that ordered for the food and the drink, when two vigilante buses sped into the property and parked. As Scorpion and his men came out from the buses, all the customers abandoned whatever they were doing and ran away. The bar owner stood petrified with the tray in her hands and stared at her customers, as they deserted her bar for fear of being harmed by the overzealous vigilante men. The vigilante men scattered tables and chairs as they marched toward Mrs. Ikedi.

"Where is your husband, woman?" asked Scorpion.

"Did Ikedi, my husband tell you that he lives in my bar, young man?" Mrs. Ikedi furiously asked Scorpion.

The vigilante men searched the bar and the surroundings and reported to Scorpion that Ikedi was not there.

One of the vigilante men kicked a table; the bottles that were on that table fell and broke into pieces. Mrs. Ikedi dropped the tray in her hands on a table ... rushed and hit the vigilante man that kicked the table.

"Stop destroying my things. Is anything the matter with you?"

The vigilante man pushed her; she pounced on him and bit him. He screamed and tried to free his flesh from her teeth, but to no avail. The moment his colleagues rushed and pulled his flesh out from the woman's teeth, the vigilante man slapped and pushed her into a chair. The chair carried her to the ground. While she wriggled in pain, Scorpion said to her, "This is lesson number one. Tell your husband that we were here."

The woman moped while the vigilante men entered their buses and drove off.

Prominent indigenes of Ogiga kingdom gathered for an emergency meeting in Isi-Ichie's compound, when *Igwe* Obi Nwako's excesses became overbearing. The most troublesome of the king's numerous sins was the manner in which he sent men of Ogiga kingdom vigilante to Ngodo town, to arrest and dehumanize Uduezue; and to attack and destroy things in Mrs. Ikedi's bar. The two acts and what led to them were seen as issues capable of sparking off war between two peaceful and friendly neighbouring communities.

"If we don't act now … and very fast for that matter," said Okoro, "this kingdom of ours that is dear to us, will go up in flame."

Some of his audience adjusted their sitting positions after he made his last statement.

Present at the meeting were Isi-Ichie, Oji, Okoro, Aghanya, Ndi-Ichie, Ozo title holders, town union executive and other members of the council of kingmakers etcetera. While they all listened attentively, Okoro informed them that the council of kingmakers had received barrages of petitions against *Igwe* Obi Nwako's high-handedness, corrupt enrichment and flagrant abuse of the constitution of Ogiga kingdom.

"*Igwe* Obi Nwako has grown so colossal, so monstrous and tyrannical that he now sits in his closet, and enact draconian laws which he enforces in this kingdom and beyond, with his army of occupation, called Ogiga kingdom vigilante. If we don't take decisive action now, this kingdom shall be engulfed by an imbroglio that will be caused by greed and other atrocious acts of one man."

Concluding, Okoro told the gathering that the council of kingmakers had invited the king twice, to clear himself from all the allegations against him and he refused to honour the invitations. He went on to say that the council of kingmakers was seeking the consent and support of all of them in that meeting so that they would commence impeachment proceedings against "His imperial majesty *Igwe* Obi Nwako." He made it known that their request was in pursuance to the powers vested in the kingmakers by the kingship constitution of Ogiga kingdom. Bowing to Isi-Ichie, he said: "*Nna anyi*, I bow." He sat down thereafter.

Isi-Ichie sought for comments and contributions when Okoro finished his address; but no one uttered a word. Instead the audience looked at each other and focused their gaze on the ground.

"With the powers vested in me as the Isi-Ichie, I unequivocally order the kingmakers to commence impeachment proceedings against *Igwe* Obi Nwako. Do not fail to sanction him if he's found culpable. That is my command."

"The kingdom has spoken," shouted his listeners with a bow.

Onochie sighted a roadblock mounted by scorpion and his men as he was driving home, after running an errand for his father, Okoro. He pulled up at the roadblock and honked his car horn repeatedly but the vigilante men felt unconcerned. Scorpion later went close to Onochie's car.

"Will you ask them to remove those things from the road?" asked Onochie, with some degree of fury.

"And when did we start taking orders from you?" asked Scorpion. "In case you're not aware, we're doing the normal security check."

"And so?" asked Onochie.

"For your information," said Scorpion, "we received a call not long ago."

"How is that my business?" asked Onochie.

"The caller told us that a vehicle ... same brand, same model and same colour with the one you are in right now, was used for robbery forty minutes ago, in this kingdom. That in effect makes you a suspect," said Scorpion.

"You must be out of your mind," retorted Onochie.

"Would you please come down for a search?"

"I can see that something is wrong with you," said Onochie, who equally chose to remain in the car instead of coming down and be searched by Scorpion and his boys.

Okoro's son never took Scorpion and his men seriously, but he became jittery when they corked their guns and pointed same at him. Scorpion opened the car's door and sternly ordered him to come down for a search. Onochie came down from the car and allowed them to search the car thoroughly. Nothing incriminating came out from the search, hence, they asked him to go. Onochie looked Scorpion in the face and said: "You must surely pay for this. I promise."

"You sound very much like your impudent father," said Scorpion.

"Even at that," said Onochie, "we are better than you folk that are armed robbers in disguise."

A vigilante man gave Onochie a tackle from behind; he fell and lay on the ground. The vigilante man placed his foot on Onochie's chest and asked: "How dare you talk to my commander with impunity?"

Later, the vigilante man removed his foot from Onochie's chest. As he was walking away, Onochie got up, rushed and tapped him on the shoulder. The vigilante man turned ... Onochie gave him a thunderous slap and a tackle. The vigilante man fell down, his gun fell off his hand and lay afar off. Onochie picked the gun from the ground and surrendered Scorpion and his men. Unfortunately for Onochie, one of the vigilante men mustered courage and shot him in the chest. He quietly fell ... Scorpion and some of his men rushed and lifted Onchie from the ground.

"He's dead," said Scorpion. "Why did you shoot him in the chest?"

Scorpion directed his question to the vigilante man that shot Onochie but the man was so shocked, to the extent that he could not answer the question. All the vigilante men rushed into their vehicles and zoomed off, when they sighted Aghanya's vehicle approaching the spot they mounted their roadblock. Aghanya pulled up at the barricade placed on the road by the vigilante men; he came down from his vehicle ... rushed and checked Onochie's pulse. He carried Onochie's corpse into his vehicle and zoomed off. While taking Onochie's body to the hospital, Aghanya made call to Okoro and asked him to come to the hospital immediately that there was an emergency that needed his urgent attention.

Aghanya sped into the hospital compound and parked at the porch. He came down from his vehicle and carried Onochie's body into the hospital's reception; and told the nurses on duty that Onochie was shot in the chest. While a nurse went to inform the doctor that there was an emergency, her colleagues led Aghanya to the emergency ward.

The doctor came into the emergency ward and took over from the nurses that were attending to Onochie. The doctor later pronounced Onochie dead; that coincided with the arrival of Okoro, Oji and four other chiefs in the ward. Okoro was shocked when he heard the doctor say that his son was dead. He moved closer to the hospital bed on which Onochie's body lay; holding his son's dead body, he screamed, "Onochie--eee!"

He lifted Onochie's dead body ... and put the deceased head on his chest and wept bitterly; while the others watched with pity. When he was asked what happened to Onochie, Aghanya told them that Onochie was shot by the vigilante men.

"Obi Nwako, you have bitten more than you can chew," said Okoro. "You've killed my only child. This certainly will be the last straw that broke the camel's back."

Okoro rushed out of the ward and slammed the door. The other chiefs tried very hard to open the door and go after him but the door proved difficult to open. The doctor and a nurse went to the door... after some trials, the nurse succeeded in opening the door.

Aghanya, Oji and the four chiefs rushed out of the ward with the intention of preventing Okoro from doing something silly. When Aghanya et al. came out from the hospital building they saw Okoro driving out from the car park in anger. They tried to stop him but he ignored them and sped out of the compound. Aghanya suggested that Oji and the four chiefs should go after Okoro while he went to Isi-Ichie's house and inform him of what the vigilante men had done to Okoro's son.

"That's a wise idea," said Oji, who instantly said to the four chiefs, "Let's go."

They all entered their respective vehicles and zoomed off. At a junction, Aghanya followed the road that led to isi-Ichie's house while Oji and the four chiefs followed the road that led to Okoro's house.

CHAPTER THIRTEEN

Okoro's car was parked in his compound while his gate was wide open when Oji and the four chiefs arrived. The chiefs drove into the compound and parked. Standing aghast after alighting from their cars, they looked round the compound and at each other before trudging toward the building. The entrance door to the house opened while the visitors were few metres away from it; Okoro burst out of the house with a pump action gun and corked it. The chiefs scurried for cover; after a while, Oji summoned courage and boldly came out from where he was hiding.

"You can't do this to yourself, Chief Okoro," said Oji.

"Get out of my way before I do something we will all regret," retorted Okoro. "*Igwe* Obi Nwako must pay for his action or my son's spirit will hunt me forever."

The four chiefs that came with Oji began to come out quietly from their hiding places. With a heart filled with pity, Oji stared at Okoro for awhile and said: "You can't take the law into your hands, Chief Okoro. If you kill Obi Nwako, you will have the law to contend with. And a man of your age and caliber cannot withstand the mockery and rigours associated with murder case."

"Where was that your law when Obi Nwako sent his renegades to kill my only child?" asked Okoro; who later tried to control the large quantity of tears streaming down from his eyes.

"But you know ... just as I do, that two wrongs don't make a right," responded Oji.

Aghanya's car sped into the compound and parked. Aghanya rushed down from the driver's seat and ran to the other side of the car; and opened the back door that was by the car's right side. Isi-Ichie alighted from the car the moment the door was opened by Aghanya. The duo headed toward Okoro after Aghanya had shut the car's door.

Okoro remained obstinate despite pleas from Oji, "Calm down, Chief Okoro. Give me the gun, please."

The four chiefs that came with Oji bowed when Isi-Ichie got close to where they stood. When Isi-Ichie got closer to Oji, he heaved a sigh, bowed and then said: "Thank God you're here, *nna anyi* [elderly one], Isi-Ichie."

Standing between Okoro and Oji, Isi-Ichie extended his hand toward Okoro ... Okoro trudged forward and grudgingly handed the gun over to him. Thereafter, he embraced and wept over the nonagenarian's shoulder. Aghanya collected the gun from Isi-Ichie and stepped aside with it. Aghanya, Oji and the four chiefs looked away in disgust as tears dropped from Isi-Ichie's eyes. Isi-Ichie comported himself and called Oji.

"I am here, *nna anyi*," answered Oji.

"Take this command," said Isi-Ichie.

Oji went and stood in Isi-Ichie's line of sight; as he bowed, he said: "Chief Oji is ready to take the command *nna anyi*."

Amidst tears, Isi-Ichie said to Oji, "Instruct the youth to take over security in the entire kingdom. All exit and entry points must be carefully and heavily guarded. Anyone coming in or going out of this town must be searched. They must ascertain the mission ... and the reasons for any movement made by anyone within and around this town. Should they encounter any problem, they must not fail to contact you through Aghanya."

"I will do exactly as you've directed," said Oji.

Isi-Ichie later called Aghanya.

Aghanya moved closer and bowed, "I am before you *nna anyi.*"

"The youth are directly under your supervision," said Isi-Ichie. "We shall hold you culpable if anything goes wrong."

"I promise never to let the kingdom down," said Aghanya; who instantly bowed to show reverence to Isi-Ichie.

Isi-ichie slid into deep thought after speaking to Aghanya. When he spoke again, he directed Oji to tell the women leader to mobilise the women to sit at the front of their compounds and at the village squares. He added that the women must not hesitate to raise alarm whenever they observed questionable movements."That is my command," he concluded.

"The kingdom wishes it," said all the chiefs as they bowed down...

Aghanya handed Okoro's gun over to one of the four chiefs that came to Okoro's compound with Oji. Afterwards, he [Aghanya] and Oji entered their respective cars and zoomed off. Isi-Ichie led Okoro into the house. The four chiefs followed them ... they shut the entrance door after they've gone into the house.

In consequence of isi-Ichie's directive, Ogiga youth armed and divided themselves into many groups. They erected barricades on all the exit and entry points to Ogiga town. The youth stopped, searched and interrogated everyone leaving or going into their town on foot or on board a vehicle. One of the groups sighted a jeep approaching their checkpoint on top speed. They began to flag it down while the jeep was still afar off.

The jeep which was occupied by three young men screeched to a stop few metres before the barricade set by the youth. The three occupants of the vehicle tried to outsmart the youth and pass without being searched; but the youth insisted on searching the jeep and its three occupants notwithstanding the trio's friendly disposition. The youth surrounded the jeep in a manner that made it impossible for the three occupants of the vehicle to escape; hence, they fidgeted.

The youth opened the vehicle's doors and ordered the three young men in it to come down. When the trio was searched, three face masks were found on them. They could not explain their reason for being in possession of those masks; neither were they able to state convincingly, their mission in Ogiga town. That gave the youth the impetus to search the vehicle thoroughly. As expected, the search yielded positive result. The youth were shocked when they discovered three pistols hidden in the jeep. They beat the three occupants of the jeep mercilessly when they failed to convincingly explain what they were doing with those guns, since they were not law enforcement officers. One of the suspects that tried to escape was given machete cut by a youth; he screamed, "Je-sus!" and fell to the ground. They tied the suspects' hands and made them sit on the ground, thereafter, youth leader brought out his mobile phone and called Aghanya; he informed him that they [the youth] had arrested three suspected robbers. Aghanya found out from him their location and told him that he was on his way to the scene.

The three suspects already had swollen eyes and faces by the time the president general of Ogiga town union got to the scene. The swollen eyes and faces were as a result of the excessive beating the suspects received from the youth. More so, the suspect that received machete cut was bleeding and groaning. After the youth leader had told Aghanya how they were able to arrest the suspects, he told them to put the bleeding suspect in the suspects' vehicle; and put the other two in his car. After his directive had been carried out, he asked the youth leader to drive the suspects' vehicle. Three youths were equally edetailed by him, to join the youth leader and the suspect with machete cut in the suspects' jeep. Aghanya equally asked three other youths to enter his car ... then, he told the others to continue with their stop and search work.

The bleeding suspect was sandwiched at the back seat of the jeep by two youths; another youth sat in passenger's seat in front, while youth leader sat on the driver's seat. Aghanya was behind the wheel in his car; a youth sat in the passenger's seat in front, while two of the suspects were sandwiched at the back seat by two other youths. Before they drove off, Aghanya called Oji on the phone and requested that the latter should come to Isi-Ichie's house immediately, that Ogiga youth had arrested some of the criminals terrorising their town.

All through their journey to Isi-Ichie's house, the suspect that received machete cut from a youth kept groaning and complaining. As a means of making him to shut up, the youths that sandwiched him smacked him each time he groaned or complained.

There was nobody in Isi-Ichie's compound when Aghanya and the youths arrived with the arrested suspects. Aghanya and the youths alighted from the vehicles they came in; later the suspects were brought down from the vehicles and were made to sit on the ground. Thereafter, Aghanya went into Isi-Ichie's house to notify him of their presence, while the youths he came with kept watch over the suspects. Aghanya was still in Isi-Ichie's house when Oji's car came into the compound and parked. Oji came out from the car with two other chiefs and headed straight to where the suspects were. Isi-Ichie and Aghanya came out from the house just as Oji got close to where the suspects were seated. Everyone except the suspects bowed when Isi-Ichie got to where the suspects were seated; thereafter, Aghanya asked the youth leader to tell Isi-Ichie where and how they arrested the suspects who were then looking remorseful.

Youth leader told Isi-Ichie the spot they erected barricade and how they searched and got three face masks on the three suspects. Isi-Ichie hummed thinking that he had heard it all; he was further shocked when youth leader told him that they equally saw three pistols hidden in the suspects' vehicle. Also the youth leader informed Isi-Ichie that the suspect with machete cut attempted to escape and was macheted by a youth to stop him from escaping. When youth leader got done with his tale, Isi-Ichie asked the suspects to tell them about themselves. One of the suspects pleaded that they should forgive them of all the atrocities they've committed against the people of Ogiga. The youths and the chiefs were surprised by what the suspect said. Shortly afterwards, Oji asked the suspects to open up to them on all the atrocities first before pleading for forgiveness.

The suspect that pleaded for forgiveness looked at his colleagues, and went on to confess that they were members off a three-man robbery gang, enlisted by *Igwe* Obi Nwako to terrorise his opponents and those he considered as potential threat to the throne. That piece of information from the suspect shook Isi-Ichie, the chiefs and the youths. They looked at each other in surprise but the suspect was not done. He equally intimated them that they were responsible for all the crime incidents recorded in the kingdom prior to their apprehension. "We are the ones that robbed Chief Oji of one of his cars and other valuables."

Oji shouted and snapped his fingers.

The people thought they've heard it all, but the suspect still had a shocker for them. "We equally kidnapped two staff of Wise-East petroleum. We shared the ransom paid for their release with *Igwe* Obi Nwako."

The people were stunned by what they heard; they shrugged and looked at each other with mouths agape. The suspect coughed and told them of their escapade in Aghanya's house. "We almost raped Chief Aghanya's wife if not for providence."

Aghanya became dismayed. He looked away immediately; wearing a dismal look, he rushed and tried to choke the life out of the confessing suspect. The youths and the chiefs rushed and freed the suspect from Aghanya's grip. Aghanya panted and stared after the suspect was freed from his grip. On his own part, the suspect held his neck with his two hands, as he coughed and panted.

Armed with green leaves, sticks, guns, and anti *Igwe* Obi Nwako placards, protesting youth of Ogiga kingdom marched toward Ogiga market junction chanting anti Obi Nwako songs. As the youth who were led by their leader marched on, vigilante men appeared in the opposite direction and started shooting in the air. Their intention was to discourage the youth from advancing further, but the youth were not deterred; they kept moving forward. The courage exhibited by the youth made the vigilante men to retreat. The vigilante men rushed into their two buses and zoomed off while the youth took over and set bonfire at the market junction.

His imperial majesty, *Igwe* Obi Nwako, *Eze Ogiliga* of Ogiga kingdom was in his sitting room watching television; and at the same time savouring delicious fruit salad, when Scorpion barged in panting. *Eze Ogiliga* was the title Obi Nwako chose for himself after his coronation.

"What is it Scorpion?" asked Obi Nwako. "Why run like someone that has seen a leopard?"

"It is worse than that your highness."

The king was shocked, "How do you mean?" he asked.

Scorpion told him that the youth were protesting; instead of showing concern, he berated Scorpion and expressed surprise that he could see youth protest as a problem. He went on to tell Scorpion that the youth were fond of staging protests and wondered why Scorpion was bothered by that day's protest.

"Your highness, this one is different," said Scorpion. "They have set bonfire at every known junction in town. We fired some shots in the air to disperse them but they kept surging forward. We ran for our dear lives; and they are on their way to the palace."

"Nonsense!" the lividly looking king shouted and stood on his feet. "That was too idiotic of you. If you've fired some shots in the air and they kept coming forward... Why didn't you shoot one or two persons or even more? ... That would have deterred them."

"Your highness, I beg to take my leave now."

"Go and do as you've been commanded."

"Yes, your highness," said Scorpion; who equally bowed and left.

Not too long after Scorpion left the king's presence, the two policemen that were detailed to protect the royal household, came in and told his royal majesty that the palace was no longer safe for him. One of the policemen was a sergeant and the other wore the rank of corporal.

"What in the name of God is the meaning of that?" was the question Obi Nwako asked the policemen.

"We just received a call from our station," said the sergeant. "There's violent demonstration in town; and we've been instructed to evacuate you and your family."

"Never!" screamed Obi Nwako. "The ground cannot run. There is violent demonstration by the youth of ogiga kingdom, but I will bring it under control in a couple of seconds."

"My colleague and I still cherish our lives," said the sergrant. "We beg to withdraw." Saluting Obi Nwako, the sergeant went on to say, "In any case we wish you luck, your highness."

The two policemen turned and were heading toward the door...

"Are you abandoning your duty post?" asked Obi Nwako.

The policemen halted and turned.

"It is only someone that is stupid that seeks collision with a moving train," said the sergeant. "Besides, I just got married. My new wife needs me dearly," the sergeant concluded and left.

"I am my parents' only child," said the corporal. "And they can't withstand the agony of childlessness if anything happens to me. Your highness, I beg to retreat."

The corporal saluted the king and exited the palace

After ruminating over the action taken by the two policemen, sent to guard him and his household, Obi Nwako brought out his phone and called the state commissioner of police. He complained to the commissioner that his men had deserted him. Instead of consoling him, the police chief shocked him by telling him that the policemen were withdrawn because of the violent protest going on in his kingdom and advised him to leave his palace immediately.

"I will quell the riot in a matter of seconds," Obi Nwako boasted; but the commissioner wasn't pacified by that. When Obi Nwako discovered that the commissioner of police was not prepared to shift his ground, he said, "All right," and quietly ended the call. He was staring at his television set when newscaster appeared on screen and said, "Here's breaking news: The police, in a short while ago arrested a notorious armed robbery suspect, Jeremi Kalajaiye; aka The Boss." The king was shocked when "The Boss" picture appeared on screen. "Je-sus!" the king shouted, and his phone fell off his hand instantly.

"The Boss" had handcuffs on his hands while he was paraded by the police.

Newscaster appeared on screen again and continued, "The suspect had been on the police wanted list for several months. Full details of the story will come your way at news time."

"Hey!" shouted a confused Obi Nwako. He stood up; his legs began to quake. "Why is my world crumbling?" he rhetorically asked. He paced about for a while … and began to think aloud. "I am finshed. I will be doomed if 'The Boss' opens up to the police. What I'm I going to do now?"

He snapped his fingers, rushed to the window and looked out in panic.

Bonfire set by the youth at market junction was still emitting smoke while the youth chanted, war songs as they headed to the palace.

Two vigilante buses appeared from opposite direction and pulled up twenty-five metres away from the protesting youth who were led by youth leader. Scorpion and his men came down from the two buses and fired some shots in the air, but the youth ignored them and kept singing and advancing.

"Hee-ey!" shouted some of the protesting youth when they discovered that Scorpion and his men had shot two of their fellow youth. They carried their shot colleagues and fearfully dispersed. The gunshot victims groaned as they were being attended to under a mango tree that was by the road side. Later on, youth leader mandated four other youths to carry the duo to the hospital. Youth leader raised a war song immediately the four youths left for the hospital with their colleagues that were shot by the vigilante men. The youth shouted, the moment their leader began to sing the war song, consequence upon that, they all raised up their weapons and moved to confront the vigilante men.

With pride, Scorpion and his men paced up and down at a particular section of the road believing that they had dispersed the youth and that fear would not allow them to stage a protest again. After a while they saw the youth furiously coming from different directions. The vigilante men released shots in the air, but the youth who had grouped themselves kept advancing. They sensed danger and rushed into their buses. As they sped through one of the youth groups, a youth threw Petrol bomb into one of the buses; the petrol bomb lifted the bus up ... when the bus was falling, it fell on the second bus; the two buses and the vigilante men in them burnt to ashes, because of the inferno that resulted from the petrol bomb thrown into one of the buses. The youth let out a loud shout of victory and continued moving forward.

A worriedly looking Obi Nwako was pacing round his sitting room when John, his driver came in with Amadi. Amadi was the driver of the king's jeep. The two drivers told their boss that they must leave the palace immediately if he still desired to live. Their show of concern irritated the king. He furiously asked them, "Are you out of your senses? ... Leave ... to where? ... I am asking you."

"Your highness, you may rant and rave at us," said John. "But, the fact remains that the youth have killed all the vigilante men; and the youth are on their way to this place ... They are even close."

Obi Nwako was stunned when he heard that the youth were close to his palace. "*E-eh!*" was the only thing that came out from his mouth. After some time, he comported himself and asked: "What did you just say?"

"You heard me right, your highness," said John. "A word is enough for the wise."

While the drivers stared, the king rushed and opened the door that led to the balcony and went out. After a while, the drivers went to the balcony to find out what the king was doing out there. Standing at the balcony, they sighted the youth afar off chanting war song and surging toward the palace with force. Obi Nwako became apprehensive; without waiting for advice, he ran back into the house. The two drivers looked at each other and shrugged before going after their master.

Obi Nwako was quaking when the two drivers came to meet him in the sitting room.

"What are we going to do now?" asked Obi Nwako.

"Your highness, at present, we have only one option," said John.

"And what could that option be?" asked Obi Nwako.

"Let's escape from this place before the mob gets here," suggested John.

John's suggestion was perfect, because that was the only action they would take if the king must live to see the next day, but Obi Nwako was skeptical; he shook his head in agony. He could not imagine himself running out of his house because of the youth, despite his enormous wealth and extensive contacts in the police and other security agencies.

"Your highness, if the youth should meet us here," said Amadi, "we're definitely going to face jungle justice."

"B-b-but," stuttered Obi Nwako, "where do we run to? And how?" he asked.

"We will escape through the back gate," said John, "and run straight to Oro River."

Obi Nwako was stunned, in his bewilderment he asked John what they were going to Oro River to do. Responding to the king's inquiry, John told him that Oro River was the boundary between Ogiga kingdom and Agba kingdom. He went on to inform his master that they would find themselves in Agba kingdom immediately they crossed the Oro River. "And the youth of Ogiga kingdom will not cross over to attack us, once we are in Agba kingdom."

"You're perfectly right, John," said Obi Nwako.

"I know you have many friends in Agba kingdom," said John. "We can take refuge in any of their houses till you sort things out."

"Thank God my children are overseas," muttered Obi Nwako. He brought out his phone and called his wife who had gone to see her uncle in the city ... and asked her to remain there until he asked her to come back.

"Let's go," he said to his drivers.

The trio rushed downstairs and escaped through the back gate while the youth fired shots in the air, and pounded on the front gate amidst chants.

About five youths scaled the fence and jumped into Obi Nwako's compound; thereafter, they broke the padlock ... and flung the main gate open. All the other youth rushed into the compound through the gate and began to break cars' glasses; also, they destroyed the windows in the king's house. After destroying the windows and breaking the car's glasses, they felt they've not done enough; because of that, they threw petrol bomb into the house and ran out of the compound. The whole house went up in flames when the petrol bomb exploded. As they watched their king's house burn, they emitted shouts of joy and congratulated each other.

Obi Nwako was later arrested by the police. He was charged with murder and armed robbery alongside "The Boss" and members of the three-man robbery gang that wore masks. After a protracted legal battle, all the suspects were convicted and sentenced to death by the court.

FROM THE AUTHOR

Thanks for finding time to read this book [Royal Audacity]. If you found it useful and interesting, please recommend it to someone else; and kindly make out time to rate and review this book in the platform you read it from.

I will be glad to read about the impression you have in relation to this book. Your recommendation will equally be appreciated. You can reach me with this email: mogorinfo@gmail.com

I'm looking forward to receiving and replying your mail.

Sincerely,

Mogor Obiorah